First an

Book One

(Featuring Jeremy Savage)

MW01103480

Coin Toss

By: Brian Amado

Introduction

Junior League Championship Game

Lincoln Eagles 27, Centerville Lions 24

4th Quarter

1:23 left......

The rain continues to drench the field as Centerville comes together to huddle at their own 45 yard line. The voice of the announcer resonates through the pouring rain, "It's been another stellar performance for Jeremy Savage as he has put together over 250 yards passing with 2 touchdowns and another 63 yards on the ground with an additional touchdown." Savage leads the Lions into the huddle and steps into the center. Inside the huddle, Savage barks out the next play to his teammates, "Here we go, strong right Z. Go on two. Ready, break!"

The Lions hustle up to the line of scrimmage, sloshing through the puddles on the field as they approach the ball. Savage takes his place under center and begins to make the calls out to the offense. "Blue 32, blue 32. Set, hut, hut."

The ball is snapped to Savage. One of the Lincoln defensive ends makes a great move on the outside and is heading straight for him. Savage spins away from the defender and sets his feet. His quick throwing motion unfolds, and suddenly the ball is rocketed out of his hand, racing towards his favorite receiver, Ricky Goodman. It is complete for a 25-yard gain. Savage turns to the ref and calls the team's second time-out of the half, leaving them with just one left for the rest of the drive. The announcer's voice comes over the speakers again, "Goodman is having a sensational day! That was his eighth catch of the game to go along with over 150 yards receiving and a pair of touchdowns."

Savage makes his way to the sidelines and approaches his coach, "What's the play, coach?"

Coach Joseph Francis has never been in this position before. In fact, prior to this year, his teams had never been any good. He had been coaching the junior league team for the past ten years in Centerville and loved every second of it, even if his teams were consistently finishing near the bottom in the standings. It wasn't his fault, though; the talent was just not on par with the bigger surrounding cities. But that all changed the day that Jeremy Savage, or "Savvy", as everyone calls him, stepped onto his practice field. From the first throw, it was obvious that the kid has incredible abilities to go along with the physical attributes that make up a great quarterback. Standing 6'2 at fourteen and still growing, Savvy is the prototypical recruit that coaches fight over. Yet, he had come, throwing perfect pass after perfect pass, to *his* practice field. If that wasn't enough, to go along with Jeremy is his best friend, Richard, or Ricky Goodman. Ricky is the fastest kid in town, and since he and Savvy have been best friends since they were little, he can catch anything that Jeremy throws. At times on the field, it looks like the two can communicate without ever saying a word.

The Lions breezed through the regular season with Savvy and Ricky dominating most of the competition, putting up video-game-style numbers never achieved before in the junior league. In the first round of the playoffs, the Lions had demolished the Claybourne Tigers, 45-7, with Jeremy throwing for four touchdowns, all to Ricky, of course, and running for the other two. In the semi-final round, the Lions once again dominated, beating the Westport Hawks, 42-14. In both of those games, Coach Francis had barely even needed to be awake as Jeremy and Ricky led the offense up and down the field with ease.

"Coach, what do you want me to go with?"

Savvy's question snaps Coach Francis back to the present. He takes a look at the plastic play sheets that he has clenched in his hands. Each sheet contains back-to-back papers, and each individual paper has a set of eight different plays, set up perfectly in squares, all designed neatly with exquisite care. The rain continues to pour down all around him, pouncing heavy droplet after droplet off of his perfectly crafted sheets.

"We are going to go with a spread set, X cross, Z 34 razor. We don't need to score right here; we just need to get close enough so that we can take a few good shots at the end zone." The coach slaps him on the helmet; Savvy nods as he takes off for the huddle awaiting him on the field.

1st and 10

Ball on the Lincoln 30 yard line

1:02 left to play

The announcer's voice expresses the weight of the moment. "Savage leads the Lions out of the huddle and scans the field. There is just over a minute to play with only one time-out left for the Lions. Here's her snap!" Savvy slides to his left, pumps once, pumps twice, and unloads a perfect spiral down the center of the field.

A Lincoln defender wraps his right arm around the receiver and uses his left hand to bat the ball away just before it falls into the hands of Savvy's running back who was streaking down the middle of the field. The running back claps his hands together in frustration as he heads back to the huddle.

2nd and 10

Ball on the Lincoln 30 yard line

:51 left to play

The Lions move up to the line of scrimmage and prepare for another attempt. Jeremy takes the snap and quickly goes through his progressions from left to right, as he has been trained to do since he was a young boy. His first read is completely covered as the Eagles elected

4

to double-team his favorite target, Ricky. His second option is also covered leaving him with only two options: throw across his body to his third option, which he has been instructed time after time not to do or...

Savage takes off to his right. He makes a great move around the corner to the twenty-five. He heads back towards the middle of the field, spins, and makes a man miss as he crosses the twenty. He gets hit and is finally brought down at the seventeen yard line. "What a tremendous run as Savage picks up thirteen much needed yards and moves his team that much closer to a championship. I have to say, folks, in all my years of calling games, I've never seen a player quite like this!"

Coach Francis calls for the team's third and final time-out and takes a long look at the wet and rumpled play sheets that are in his hands. He knows that he needs to make the right call. In all honesty, this may be the only time he ever gets the chance to win the league championship. He does not want to let it all slip away in the waning seconds.

"Jeremy, we are going to free-up Ricky with the trips formation, wheel route. Run it right, and we should be good to go. Remember, you have done this a hundred times before in practice...you got this." Savvy delivers the call and leads his team out of the huddle.

1st and 10
Ball on the Lincoln 17 yard line

:32 left to play

The ball is snapped and Savage takes his drop back. Goodman swings around the right end and sprints up the right sideline. Savage sets his feet and makes his read. He fires the ball down the right sideline and hits Goodman at the 5. He is stopped from going out of bounds and is downed at the 3-yard line.

"The Lions have to hurry up to the ball as the clock continues to run down. 20, 19, 18 seconds...they have got to stop the clock to have a chance!"

The Lions get up to the 3 yard line. The referee spots the ball as the clock continues to tick down. The ball is snapped and Jeremy spikes the ball into the ground at the 4-yard line, stopping the clock with 12 seconds left to play.

"This is it folks! 12 seconds left to go in the game and the Lions are threatening on the Eagle 4-yard line. Can Savage lead the Centerville Lions to their first ever Junior League Championship? Or will the mighty Eagles defend their title for a third straight season?"

1st and Goal
Ball on the Lincoln 4 yard line
:12 left to play

Savvy takes a quick look to the right and then the left as he gets ready to go under center. He notices that the defense is staggered to the left, most likely because they are going to shift double coverage to Ricky. He taps his foot, sending the running back into motion. The running back sprints to the left side of the formation and lines up. To compensate, the outside linebacker shifts into coverage, and the middle linebacker swings to the open spot. Jeremy notices that the other linebacker does not shift into position to fill the hole.

The ball is hiked from the center to Savage. He takes a quick step back. (10 seconds, 9 seconds to go.) He pulls the ball down, and tucks it away as he heads upfield. (7 seconds, 6 seconds.) He sees a hole as the right guard makes a great block. Savage is hit at the 1, spins away, and stretches the ball across the goal line.

"He's in!! Savage has crossed the goal line for the second time today as the Lions take the lead over the Eagles, 30-27. What an incredible effort by this quarterback!"

As Jeremy is helped up by his teammates, he squints through the rain and wind to see the scoreboard read 30-27. There are only 2 seconds left on the clock.

Following the game, Jeremy Savage racked up yet another championship along with a trophy to add to his already impressive assortment. Of course, he would be named MVP of the championship and another piece of hardware would be added to his ever-expanding collection. He has been groomed to be a champion since he was a little boy. It's what is expected of him.

What he was not ready for were the challenges that awaited him..

1

"You've got to catch that, man!" Jeremy shouts in the direction of his friend Ricky. The football hits the ground and bounces at odd angles for a few seconds before stopping. Ricky quickly jogs over to the ball and picks it up.

"That was a terrible throw. For me to catch it, you have to put it near me," Ricky hollers back to Jeremy as he throws the ball to him. He makes his way back to Jeremy and lines up again. "What do you want me to run this time?"

"Same thing...we do it until we get it right. Ready, go!" Ricky takes off, sprints ten yards, plants his right foot in the turf and angles upfield, running a post route. Jeremy takes his typical three-step drop and starts to count off in his head, "One thousand one, one thousand two, one thousand three." He knows that the ball has to be out of his hand before he makes it to four. As he gets to three, he sets his back foot and begins the flawless throwing motion that has been perfected through countless hours of practice. The ball launches out of his hand like it's been shot out of a cannon. It sails through the air in a perfectly tight spiral, heading towards its intended destination. Ricky pumps his legs faster and stretches out his arms as the ball falls into his hands.

"That's what I am talking about, that's how you catch that ball!"

Ricky cradles the ball and takes a few more strides before slowing down and eventually stopping. He turns to look at Jeremy,

"Savvy, that was a better pass. You put it anywhere near me and I'll catch it. That last throw was way off target, my friend." Ricky smiles wide and begins to run back to Jeremy. "I mean, seriously, you know how many times I have had to save your butt in games?"

"Save me? Now I know you've gone crazy. Maybe it's the heat or the sun, but something is doing some damage to your brain." Ricky throws the ball back to Jeremy and switches things up by lining up on the left. "All right QB, what's up next?"

"You look like you might be a little winded. Maybe we should run some short stuff for a little while to let you catch your breath?"

"Catch my breath! Please! I could do this all day. What's next?"

"Ok if you say so...how about we run a fade. I' m going to put the ball just over your head and hit you in stride right in the hands." Jeremy holds the ball out in front of him and yells, "hike." Again, Ricky takes off, running at full speed, drifting slightly to the left as he streaks up field. Jeremy begins the silent count in his head as he has been taught to do and lets the ball fly. It soars through the sky, cutting through the air at just the right height and angle. Ricky puts his hands out and the ball lands effortlessly into them for what would have been a sure touchdown.

A loud clapping sound behind him makes Jeremy's head snap around. A large man, standing well over six feet tall with short cropped, but meticulously maintained, brown hair continues to clap as he makes his way over to where Jeremy is standing. Even from the distance,

10

Ricky can tell exactly who the man is without needing to see his face. Coach Robert Fletcher or "Coach Fletch" as his players call him, strides up to Jeremy with a wide smile on his face. The sun reflects brightly off his Ray Ban sunglasses, and his immaculate polo shirt, navy blue with white stripes, looks impressive and expensive. On the left hand side of the shirt is the school's mascot, the falcon, with St. Michael's printed above it and Falcons below it.

"That was a great pass Jeremy. You know, that's not an easy throw to make, but you sure do make it look simple." The coach turns to face the receiver 40 yards away. He holds up a hand and begins to wave. "That you out there, Ricky? I know it must be you. Who else could make a great catch like that look so easy?" Coach Fletch is notorious for consistently having great teams and finding a way to get all of the best players from the area to come to his school to play. In reality, everyone knows that St. Michael's Preparatory School is the best place to go if you are an athlete. Most kids drool over the thought of having Coach Fletch come and talk to them about attending St Michael's to play football. Who could argue with his credentials or his results?

Robert Fletcher had been a high school superstar at St. Michaels in the early nineties and won two state titles there. He led the league in every statistical category a quarterback could and set a number of state records along the way. He earned a full scholarship to a Division I school where he played well and earned himself a spot on a professional roster, which is unheard of coming from the Centerville area. He kicked around as a professional for a few years before coming back home to take the head coach's position at his alma mater, St. Michaels.

St. Michaels had always been good, but when they got the legendary Robert Fletcher to coach the team, every kid wanted to play for them. Since this was the case, it was easy to see how Coach was able to assemble teams loaded with the best talent. In the twelve years he has been coaching the team, they have made the playoffs every year, winning ten district championships and four state titles. It is quite a resume for any coach, not to mention one that has only been on the job for twelve seasons. With all that, here he stands, clapping and grinning in front of Jeremy with that award-winning smile and perfectly whitened teeth.

"Why don't you come on in here, Ricky. I'd like to talk to you and Jeremy for a little bit."

The coach turns to face Jeremy, "Let me properly introduce myself. My name is Coach Fletcher, but everyone on my team calls me Coach Fletch. I'd like it if you would do the same." He holds out a hand, Jeremy accepts it, and shakes it firmly. "I know who you are coach, everybody does."

"Wow, you sure got a strong grip there son. Sign of strong hands. You know, every quarterback needs to have strong hands." Jeremy shrugs off the compliment just as Ricky walks up next to him.

"Hey coach. My name is Ricky Goodman." Ricky stretches out his and the coach grabs it and shakes it with both of his hands. "You kidding me? Ricky Goodman, the kid who caught a pair of touchdowns in the Junior Championship game. Of course I know who you are." Jeremy can tell that Ricky is a little caught up in the excitement of actually meeting the coach face-to-face. This is something that Ricky has talked about for years, gushing over the coach as if he were some sort of movie star or something.

A serious look sweeps over the Coach's face. He holds his hands out directly in front of his chest. With his right hand, he begins to twist a ring located on his left hand around and around. The sun reflects brightly off the shiny gold of the ring as Jeremy analyzes it. From the inscription on the ring, Jeremy is able to determine that the ring is from the last state title won by St. Michael's.

The Coach begins, "Listen boys, I'm going to get straight to the point. I want you both to come and play for me at St. Michaels in the fall. Everyone is well aware of the talent you two have. I'm also sure that you both are aware of the fact that my program has produced multiple state titles as well as a wealth of scholarship athletes that have gone off to play football at some of the best colleges in the country. Before either of you say anything, I also think that it's important you know that I fully believe that you both can come in and play right away. We have a need at the quarterback position and Ricky, I think you could come in and contribute to the team this year at the varsity level."

Saying that St. Michaels has a need at quarterback is a bit of a stretch. Granted, the starting quarterback from last year graduated and the second man on the depth chart, who is going to be a junior this year, really does not have the gifts that Jeremy has, but the kid is no chump and can start at pretty much any other high school in the state. "I know what you are thinking, Jeremy. We already have a quarterback that's an upperclassman and knows the system. While that may be true, we really feel that you have the tools and abilities to come in and start this season for us at the varsity level."

"I appreciate that Coach, and I'm not going to lie to you, playing for you is something that's crossed my mind more than once. However, I also want to play at the highest level that I can, and I know that if I go to Centerville High, I'll start varsity right away."

"I figured as much. That's why I wanted it to be clear that we want you to start this season for us." The thought of starting varsity as a freshman at St. Michaels is not something that Jeremy figured was even possible. Typically, there is so much solid talent there that most kids don't even really get a shot at varsity until they are sophomores or juniors.

"We're in!" The words fly out of Ricky's mouth so fast he doesn't even consider what his friend might think about the offer.

Ricky has been waiting years for this. Every day that he trains and every pass he catches has all led him to this moment. All of the working out, the eating right, the endless hours of training has all been for this day: the day when Coach Fletch would ask him to play for the mighty St. Michael's Falcons.

Jeremy's head jerks around quickly. The fire in his eyes burns right through Ricky's enthusiasm and makes him slightly shrink away from his friend.

"Listen coach, I really appreciate the offer, but I need to think about it, ok?"

"It's a smart decision not to rush into something; however, I can tell you that St. Michael's is the best place for you boys. You want to take your game to the next level? You want to get a full scholarship to a big-time school? You want to play for a state championship year after year? If you do, St. Michael's can offer all of that to you." The coach's eyes move from Jeremy to Ricky. "So, it sounds like you are interested in coming to play for me in the fall. I'm glad to hear it. With your speed and skills, you'll be a star at St. Michael's in no time." Ricky smirks and takes a step forward, extending his hand, but Jeremy cuts him off before he reaches the coach.

"Don't you think it may be a good idea to run this by your father first?" Ricky's voice lowers so that only Jeremy can hear him, "My dad doesn't care what I do anymore. You know that. He hasn't cared for years."

"Still, you don't think this is something you want to talk to him about before you accept?"

"I'll be lucky if he's sober when I get home, nevermind able to have an actual conversation."

Ricky's dad was sort of a mess, but his dad hasn't always been like that. In fact, he and Jeremy's dad used to be really great friends. Years ago, the two families spent lots of time together. Then there was the accident.

One night Ricky's parents had gone out to dinner for their tenth wedding anniversary. When Ricky woke up, he was told that his parents had been involved in a major car accident. His mother had died instantly, and his father was in critical condition at the hospital. The details of the accident were a little sketchy, but the police were able to determine that a group of three college students had done a little too much partying and had blown through a red light. Their car, driving well above the posted speed limit, slammed into Ricky's parents' SUV with extreme force. The three students escaped the accident with bumps, bruises, and a few broken bones, while Ricky's dad had to fight for his life. When they told Ricky's dad what had happened to his wife, a big part of him died. Ever since the accident, his bright blue eyes had lost the glimmer that they once had. He never smiled anymore. He wasn't able to work and had a very noticeable limp. The settlement from the accident had been a pretty hefty sum, but it was nothing compared to what they had lost that day. Ricky's dad's life seemed to end the day of that accident. He stopped going to Ricky's games and practices and stopped caring about himself entirely.

16

One day when he was, once again, noticeably drunk, Jeremy asked him why he drank so much. He replied that he felt like he had a huge hole inside of him, and the only thing that he could fill it with was booze. After that, Jeremy's parents stopped letting him go to the house and started inviting Ricky over more and more. Now, they were almost at the point where Jeremy's parents really were Ricky's parents.

Ricky takes a long look at his friend and considers his words. Although this is exactly what he has wanted for as long as he could remember, Jeremy is right about his dad.

"Coach, I'm positive I want to go to play for you, but Jeremy is right. I guess I should talk to my dad first."

The Coach smiles. Getting parents to see the benefits of their child attending St. Michael's is something he has perfected. Mothers like him because he is handsome and a quasi-celebrity in the area. Fathers love him even more because he can talk football all day and dish out stories from his college and professional days. It also doesn't hurt that St. Michael's has an excellent reputation for academics. They boast about their 100 percent graduation rate as well as the impressive list of colleges and universities that their former students attend. Just this past year, out of a class of 225, they had over 20 students get accepted into Ivy League schools and another 15 receive full Division I athletic scholarships. Everybody knows that on St. Michael's college day, all of the best schools come to set up booths in hopes of grabbing some of the most talented and gifted of America's youth. Bottom line, if you attend St. Michael's you have the best chance for future success, and the coach knows this. He not only knows it, he understands exactly how to use all of that information to get precisely what he wants.

"Ricky, here's my card. Have your dad give me a call anytime, and I'll come by and discuss all of the things St. Michael's has to offer a superior athlete like yourself." The coach opens his brown leather wallet, takes out two glossy business cards. He hands one to Ricky and one to Jeremy. "Same goes for you too, Jeremy. I'd love to come to the house and sit down with your folks. I know talent when I see it, and you have the stuff it takes to get all the way to the pros, as long as you're willing to work hard enough and make the right choices." The coach slides the wallet back into his pocket and turns his well-tanned face up, embracing the warmth of the sun. "Well, I'm going to let you boys get back to it. Make sure your parents give me a call." With that, he turns and walks away, leaving the two of them standing there holding the business cards.

"Holy crap! Holy crap!" Ricky just keeps shouting the same phrase over and over. He's holding the coach's business card in his hands like he's holding a check for a million dollars.   "Ricky you shouldn't have done that."

"Done what?"

"I don't know if I want to go to St. Michael's. I was thinking about maybe just staying with all of our friends and going to Centerville High."

"You're joking, right? Dude, they suck! They have been terrible since we were little. They are always going to suck because anyone that's any good from Centerville goes to St. Michael's, just like the two of us are going to do. This way, we don't have to play with guys that aren't any good!"

"The guys that play aren't that bad; we just won the championship with those guys."

"Are you nuts? That's because of us, you wacko! Without us, that team is nothing. We made that team what it is and you know that. Without us they don't even get close to the championship round."

"That team was pretty good. I thought our defense played really well."

Ricky scoffs, "I'm confused. Centerville's junior league team has never won anything. Then we are on the team and boom! Championship!" Jeremy reaches to the ground and picks up the football. He stands there spinning the ball around in his right hand for a bit while Ricky continues to ramble. "Think of this. Who is going to play running back for us next year if we go to Centerville? The kid that's there now is terrible and, without a running game, the defenses are going to key in on the passing game."

"What about Chuck? He's pretty good at running back, don't you think?"

Ricky bursts out laughing, "Chuck? He's lucky if he makes it to junior varsity, nevermind varsity. He's so slow! I can run faster than that

19

kid going backwards. Now, at St. Michael's they have that Gomes kid that ran all over the place this past year. You put him together with us, and we would be unstoppable. We'll set every offensive record there is together and cruise right to the state title."

Jeremy stops spinning the ball and thinks for a moment about the possibility of playing with other great players. His whole life, he has always been the best. Well, he and Ricky. They were the best at every sport. It didn't matter what it was: Basketball, baseball, football, soccer, you name it, they dominated it. At least, they dominated in their small town of Centerville against their friends. Going to St. Michael's would be a whole new ball game. All the kids that play at St. Michael's were the best in their towns too.

Jeremy had to admit that Ricky was making good points. Centerville isn't exactly turning out high-caliber sports talent on a regular basis. What it does have going for it is that it is an absolutely beautiful small town in New England. Although St. Michael's is only about an hour's ride away, it's located in the heart of one of the biggest cities in the state, which is a stark contrast to Centerville. Centerville has a modest population of around 40,000 residents, but you can get to the beach in fifteen minutes from anywhere in the town.

Jeremy loves the fact that here, one can fully experience all four seasons. Fall is his favorite and not just because of football. During fall, the leaves changed from bright and bold green to beautiful bouquets of reds, oranges, and yellows, which remind Jeremy of the stunning colors

20

you see during a fireworks show. He also has a love for snowboarding and doesn't mind the fact that he can get to a mountain within only a few hours. Spring can be a bit of a downer as it often rains and seems to quickly transition from cold to hot. The summer is when Jeremy gets a lot of his prep work done for the upcoming football season. He trains very hard during these long, hot days and uses every second of daylight he can.

As Jeremy continues to ponder all of this, Ricky takes off running straight. "Hit me, I'm open!" Jeremy locks in on his target and quickly considers all of the variables: speed, wind, and trajectory. He grins and releases a tight, perfect spiral that slices through the air and hits Ricky exactly where he wants it to go; on the right side of his body, low enough so it is easy to catch but in a location where a defender can't knock it down.

As he stands there and waits for Ricky to run the ball back in to him, he can't help but contemplate the offer to play at St. Michael's. How would it feel to be able to throw to three or four guys that can catch a ball as well as Ricky? If he plays with the best of the best, would more Division I schools come to scout his games? Jeremy has to admit that the answers to these questions seem clear.

2

Coach Robert Fletcher opens the door to his brand new black luxury SUV and takes a seat. The supple leather of the chair is comfortable and inviting. The meeting with Jeremy and Ricky seemed to have gone well, and he is feeling pretty confident that he will be able to land both players. Truth be told, Jeremy is really the main attraction out of the two, but why not grab a solid athlete with great speed while he's at it? He puts the car into drive and sets off towards home. He has a few hours of film to comb over before he meets with the next recruit, a running back with blazing speed out of a nearby town called Adamsville.

The coach cruises along the highway on the near hour-long ride home. His cell phone vibrates to life. He pushes the button on his car's built-in receiver to initiate the blue tooth sequence. The car's system picks up the phone call and a small microphone built into the car transmits his voice. "Hello, this is Coach Robert Fletcher."

"Robert, so nice to talk to you again," says the man. "Are you busy at the moment?"

Robert recognizes the man's voice. It is the mayor of Centerville. "Hello, Mr. Mayor. I'm on my way home right now to watch some video on a new recruit, but I think that I can spare a few minutes of my time for the mayor of Centerville. What can I do for you?"

"Robert, this is something I would prefer that we discuss in person. Would you mind coming over to my house?" Robert is a little taken aback by the question. Although he does not live in Centerville, he does not live far from it. He knows that the mayor's reach extends far beyond the town's borders. "Yes, sir. I'm most likely not that far from you right now. Just text the address, I'll be there shortly."

"Excellent, see you soon." The mayor hangs up the phone and punches a few buttons on it before setting it down on his desk. He looks at the men sitting at various places in the room. "He's on his way."

The collection of men, representing the wealthiest members of Centerville's elite, have been relentlessly badgering him for the past few hours. Normally, he would simply placate them, promising that he would surely look into whatever they are asking for. He had even offered to take the matter directly to the Athletic Director of the town, but that wasn't good enough. They want him to deal with it personally. For the first time, the men are threatening to remove something that he knows is most vital to his future success.

One of the men casually takes a sip from his drink before he speaks, "I don't know about the rest of you, but I'm tired of that smug Coach Fletcher coming into our town and poaching our talent, but I can't blame the kids for wanting to go to St. Michael's. My son is going to be a sophomore this year, and he has already lost a number of friends

23

because they have elected to go to St. Michael's or other private schools in the area. I've got half a mind to send him there myself if our school programs do not begin to show some growth. "

Sitting quietly next to the man that just spoke are two other men. They are brothers, although most do not see the resemblance readily. One of the brothers clears his throat audibly before addressing the mayor, "My brother and I have invested a lot of money into your previous campaigns. As of right now, we are contemplating contributing this year as well. You have been instrumental in removing some of the, shall we say, pit falls, that have cropped up from time to time over the last few years. However, before we can fully pledge ourselves to this campaign, we are going to need some assurances from you regarding your commitment to certain things at the high school."

The other brother picks up the conversation, "We do not care about anything other than this. *You* need to find a way to keep the young talent we have from leaving the area. *You* need to find a way to ensure my brother and I, as well as the people in this room, that you are going to do anything and everything in your power to keep Jeremy Savage in Centerville. This is a problem that we need you to work on immediately or else, when you come asking for your next donation, you will learn what it is like to campaign without our funding."

The brothers stand up and begin to walk out of the room. Before they do, the first brother turns to say one last thing, "It all starts with this boy, Jeremy. You get him to stay; you will see the sports programs

24

ascend, which is what everyone in this room collectively wants. Oh, and while you are at it, fire that head coach at Centerville. The man is a born loser." With that, the two exit.

As the door to the office closes behind the brothers, the rest of the group is beginning to get restless. "Clinton, the bottom line is that we want our kids to have some pride in the school they attend and frankly, right now, they just don't. It's tough for me to explain to my daughter why her school can't be really good at any one thing. You need to step in and do something, now. Keeping that kid in Centerville is a giant step in the right direction to show us that you are taking this matter seriously. I caution you, if you do not take the concerns that have been voiced here to heart, then I think you will find yourself on the outside looking in after this years' election."

For the first time in his political career, the mayor is feeling pressure. To this point, he has been able to coast to easy victories, shoring up enough money to crush his competition in convincing fashion. Now, with the threat of losing some of or all of that money, he knows that he may lose what he holds most dear: power.

The doorbell chimes loudly throughout the house. A woman opens the door to see an attractive man staring back at her. "Hello, I'm Coach Fletcher. The mayor called. I guess he wants to see me?" The woman smiles, "Yes, Coach Fletcher. He is expecting you. Please, follow me, and I'll take you right to him." The two walk down a long hallway and eventually come to a closed set of double doors. She knocks on the door and waits for a reply. "Come in" comes from within.

Coach Fletcher follows the woman into the room. "Mr. Mayor, Coach Fletcher has arrived to see you."

"Thank you, Courtney. That will be all for now."

Courtney smiles and shuts the door behind her. Coach Fletcher walks into the room and sees a gathering of excessively well-dressed men. The Coach walks over and extends a hand towards the mayor. "Hello, sir. It's a pleasure to see you again."

"It's a pleasure to see you again as well, Coach. Please, have a seat. Let me introduce you to a few of the people here. You already know Mr. Wilson Pemberton, the owner of Pemberton Country Club here in Centerville. This is Clyde Rainsworth, a longtime supporter and friend of mine. The other gentlemen you see are Gregory Hollinsworth, Colin Granderson, and Joseph Giancarlo. These men are some of my constituents from Centerville. They each have a vested interest in what we are about to discuss. "

The coach smiles and nods his head towards the group of men. "It's a pleasure to see you again, Mr. Pemberton. It's nice to meet you, Mr. Rainsworth, and hello to the rest of you as well."

"Coach, I asked you here for one reason, so I'm just going to get right to it. I need you to stop your recruiting of Jeremy Savage. I really need him to attend Centerville High in the Fall. Now, before you say anything, I know that you like to come into Centerville and sweep away

26

all of my talent and whisk them off to St. Michael's. Usually, I just sit back idly and allow you to do as you please. Just not this time; not this kid."

The mayor's words are pointed, leaving little room for debate. The coach smirks, feeling a little uneasy. "You're joking, right? I don't mean to be disrespectful, sir, but I don't owe you anything, and I'm not about to take orders from you either." The coach shifts agitatedly in his seat; he can feel his adrenaline pumping. Why should he kowtow to this man? The mayor has friends, sure, but so does he. You don't get to be the most respected coach in the state, the coach of a very exclusive preparatory school, without making a number of friends along the way.

Sweat is beginning to bead up on the mayor's forehead. He needs to demonstrate to the men in the room that he can get this done. His voice increases in intensity, "Listen, Robert. I'm not really asking you; I'm more telling you what it is that I need from you. In turn, I'll do you a favor down the road. This is how things get done in the world."

Although the mayor had not wanted to issue any threats, the coach is proving to be less than accommodating to his request. This is something that the mayor simply cannot have happen to him right now, not in front of these men.

"Robert, you know who I am. You know that I can throw around my political weight with the best of them. Do you really think it wise to not work with me on this?"

The coach, now enraged, shoots up out of his chair, knocking it to the ground in the process, "I know others are afraid of you, but I'm not. I have friends in high places too. I came here out of courtesy, and you treat me like I'm some sort of runt you can push around. Guess what. I'm not. I'm not taking my foot off the gas pedal when it comes to Jeremy. I want him on my team, a real team, not that sad excuse of a football team over at Centerville High." The blood is rocketing through his veins as his voice continues to escalate in intensity and volume. "Who do you think that you are? Seriously? You think that you can bully me? The coach takes a few angry steps towards the mayor.

Clyde leaps out of his seat and stands directly in the coach's path. "Take one more step, and I promise you, you will not like the result." The way he says these words makes the coach stop dead in his tracks. "I'll tell you what. I've already made my pitch to the kid. Let's see what you can do. He can either play for the best program in the state, or he can play for Centerville and see what's it's like to finish at the bottom with the rest of the riffraff." The coach storms out of the room, violently slamming the door on his way out.

Clyde stands there calmly while Wilson rises to his feet. Clyde faces the mayor and speaks in a very controlled tone, "You are going to have to find a way to get that boy to play at Centerville, yet you have exceptionally little to offer. I suggest you look to Jeremy's parents." Clyde bows his head slightly towards Wilson and leaves.

Wilson looks the mayor dead in the eyes. "Clinton, I'm going to make this very easy for you. Either get the kid, or I am out as a financial backer for this campaign." Following his words, Wilson and the rest of the men depart the room, leaving the mayor sitting alone.

The mayor is livid, but he knows that he needs to keep a clear head and think. He picks up his phone and dials. "What do you need?" says a voice on the other end of the line.

"I need you to look into David and Jessica Savage for me. Find me everything you can, I want to know what they like, what they hate, what they eat, the works. I need to know what makes them tick, I need something that I can use, do you understand?"

"Standard rate?" asks the voice on the other end.

"Yes, I'll pay you the standard rate. Just do as I ask." With that, the mayor ends the call. Without the financial support of Wilson and the brothers, his political career will be ruined. More than that, the parents in the community are also threatening to pull their support for him if he doesn't deliver. He stares blankly at the ceiling and hopes desperately that the person on the other end of that call will be able to find something useful.

3

Jeremy tosses his duffel bag on the floor as he walks into the house and shuts the door. His mother pokes her head out from the kitchen, "Hey honey, where's Ricky? I thought he was coming by for dinner."

"He went home first. He's going to come by later." Jeremy stretches and then makes his way into the kitchen.

"You know that you are going to take a shower before we eat, right?

Jeremy rolls his eyes, "Yeah, I know mom."

"Something came in the mail for you today. It's over on the counter." Jeremy strolls to the fridge and grabs a bottle of water. He twists off the cap and drinks the entire bottle in one big gulp. "Ahh, that's the good stuff." He tosses the bottle into the recycling bin and walks over to the counter. He picks up the envelope and turns it over in his hands. As soon as he sees the insignia on the top, left-hand, corner, he knows exactly what it is. He hurriedly rips it open and begins to read aloud,

Dear Jeremy Savage,

It is our pleasure to invite you to the week-long camp sponsored by Direct Athletics Performance. As you may already know, Direct Athletics Performance extends this offer only to the best young athletes from around the country. This week-long camp will provide you the

opportunity to work with well-known coaches and trainers, as well as provide you with the chance to compete against and with some of the best talent the country has to offer. On the subsequent pages you will find your application form, medical release form, itinerary, and travel instructions. We look forward to seeing you soon!"

Sincerely,

Kenneth Davis

Director of Student Athlete Relations

Direct Athletic Performance

Jeremy looks up at his mom, his hands still quivering with excitement. "Do you know what this means?"

"Not really, but I'm guessing from your reaction that this is a really good thing."

He runs over to his mom and gives her a huge hug, lifting her off her feet. He swings her around in a circle and places her back down. "Mom, if you get invited to this camp, it means that you are the best of the best. More than that, it means that *they* think that you are the best of the best. There will be representatives from all of the major recruiting services like Rivals.com and ESPN! If I do well there, the people that put out the high school player rankings will know my name before I even start high school. It's the opportunity of a lifetime! They only invite a few kids at each position to go. I can't believe they want me!"

Just then, Jeremy hears the garage door open, indicating that his father is home. He is bursting with excitement and can't wait to tell his dad about meeting the coach as well as the invitation he has just received. "Wait till I tell dad! He's going to go nuts!" Jeremy runs over to the door that leads to the garage and whips it open, "Dad, you're never going to believe this!"

The funny thing is, Jeremy knows that his father is not only going to believe it, he has been expecting it. David Savage had been a pretty good athlete back in his day. He lettered in both football and baseball and was captain of both teams as a senior. He had a very good, (but not great) arm, but was a smart player. He played quarterback for the football team and pitched for the baseball team. He had dreamed of being a professional athlete, but he knew that the talent just wasn't there. As a senior, he was able to draw some interest from a few local Division III colleges and played baseball for all four years at one of them. It was at this school that he met his future wife, Jessica Quinn.

Jessica was a tennis player and had been in the weightroom one afternoon getting ready for her season. David was doing a light workout before hitting the books to study for a final when he bumped into her. He was hooked after the first glimpse. He graduated with a degree in education and became a teacher at the local middle school. They married a few years later and two years after that, Jeremy was born. They tried to have a second, but it just never worked out for them so they decided to stop trying and be happy with the one son that they felt lucky to have.

32

His father is his biggest supporter; he had been the one that recognized Jeremy's ability to throw, even when he was a little boy. His father is the one that worked extra to be able to afford the throwing coaches and strength trainers that his mother thought were unnecessary. He is the one that always takes him to practice and plays catch with him outside, even when he is exhausted after work. His father does all this because he truly believes in his son and wants him to be put in the best possible place to succeed.

"What's all the excitement about, Buddy?" His father asks as he shuts the car door and puts the strap of his bag over his shoulder.

"I got invited, Dad. I just got the letter."

"That's great son. Invited to what?" His father puts an arm around Jeremy and walks him into the kitchen. He inhales deeply, "Whew! Hey, Buddy, I think you may want to take a shower."

"I told you that you needed one," his mother says over the sizzling pans on the stove.

"Yeah, I'll take one in a second. Dad, I got invited to the Direct Athletics Performance Camp."

His father put his bag down and smiles broadly, "I knew you were going to get it. Didn't I tell you they were going to invite you?" His father pumps his fist in the air and then gives Jeremy a light slap on the back. "Great job. I told you that you're *that good*, didn't I? His father runs over to his wife and gives her a big kiss. "You see our boy over there? He's going to go to college for free! F-R-E-E, that spells free!"

"He's not even in high school yet, David. What are you talking about?"

"The camp he's talking about is put on by Direct Athletics Performance. They are a very well-known organization that is used by many professional athletes to get ready for their seasons. It doesn't matter what the sport; the best always train at this place. They make a ton of money and are very well-respected by college and professional organizations everywhere. As a way of giving back a little, they put on a camp for all of the four major sports, one week each, in the summer. This is strictly an invitation-only type of thing; not just anyone can go to this. At the camp, the kids get to work with the best in the industry, from trainers to position coaches, and they get to utilize all of the amenities the professional athletes pay to use. I've never seen the inside, but I'm sure it's absolutely incredible."

"I don't understand. What's in it for the people putting on the camp?"

"Honey, in this day and age, it's all about what college is putting out the best athletes, where does this guy train so I can train there, what supplements does that guy take so I can take the same, and so on and so on. For the organization, not only do they get to say that "so and so" went to this camp and now look, he's a big deal, but also, when these guys are professionals, who do you think they are going to remember

34

when it's time to pick a place to train during the offseason? Not only will those guys want to come back to train there, but, guess what? Now, they have money."

David realizes that he's talking at a pretty quick pace and suddenly feels like he needs to take in a breath. Jeremy uses this opportunity. "Dad, that's not all. Coach Fletch came to see me and Ricky today. He wants us to play for him." His father knows exactly what these two things mean for his son's future and can't help but feel overwhelming pride. "You've earned all of these things, Jeremy. All the hard work, the dedication, the late nights throwing the ball-it's all led to this right here. You're going to go to this camp to show off your skills and you also have the opportunity to play for the best program in the area."

"So, you think I should play for St. Michaels? Should I even consider Centerville?" Jeremy's dad walks over to him and looks him in the eyes, "I know you are going to miss some of your friends, but this is a real opportunity for you. You are going to play with the best of the best, and when you shine like I know you will, everyone's going to take notice. At St. Michael's you are going to have the opportunity to win, year-after-year. Not only that, but you know Coach Fletcher has contacts all over the country. The decision is ultimately yours, but I really think this is kind of an easy one to make."

Jeremy thinks about all of the kids on his junior league team. He has been playing on the same team with most of them since he was just a little boy in pee wee football, and he really likes a lot of them. Brett Rose played tight end and some linebacker for the team this past year. He is a really funny kid that always makes jokes and has the coolest parents ever. Jeff Sanders, one of the wide receiver/cornerbacks, is absolutely crazy all the time and constantly does the most ridiculous things just to make people laugh. Walter Jefferies, who didn't really play very much, is, by far, one of the most interesting characters Jeremy has ever met. He is pretty overweight but incredibly bright. In school, everyone calls him "genius" or "whiz kid." Walter is the best at every video game Jeremy has ever played with him. Walter is always the first in line to buy any new game on the day that it comes out, no matter the cost. His father is some sort of real estate tycoon and owns properties all over the country. They have a ton of money, and Walter gets whatever he wants. Jeremy guesses that it is an attempt to make up for the fact that he is never around. Walter is a master of on-line gaming and dominates every competition in all facets, especially all the first-person shooting games. In fact, he is so good that the only way any of the guys will play with him is if they can play on the same team. Other than that, it is simply no fun to play with Walter. You might think that other kids would poke fun at Walter because he is super smart and a little heavy, but not with Zach Hayes around you don't.

Zach Hayes was an offensive and defensive lineman on the team this past season and is a complete fitness nut. The kid works out all the time and has bigger muscles than most grown men. He is the first person Jeremy calls if he wants to hit the gym because Zach is always up for pumping a little iron, even if he has already gone to the gym that day. Zach likes to have fun and makes cracks about how weak everyone else is compared to him, but he does it in a playful way. He was bullied when he was really little because he was the smallest kid in class up until sixth grade. Then, he had a growth spurt and started to work out a little. Now, he is a monster compared to the other kids in school. If he ever sees someone getting picked on, he stands up for them. It doesn't matter if he knows the kid or not, you are not going to bully someone in front of Zach, especially Walter. It is one of the things Jeremy admires most about Zach. Although it seems like he and Walter have nothing in common, for some reason they are the best of friends and hang out together all of the time. Walter even tutors Zach sometimes when he really doesn't get something in math class.

Then there is Jake Houston. Jake played linebacker and also plays the guitar, which Jeremy thinks is pretty cool. Larry Torino is the guy that everyone on the team calls the ladies' man. Every time you see Larry at practice or at school, he seems to be talking to or holding hands with a different girl. Here's the crazy part: it is always one of the best-looking girls the guys have ever seen. Larry looks like he could be a kid movie star. He has perfect sandy blonde hair and striking blue eyes. He seems to have a perfect year-round tan and keeps himself in good shape thanks to all the sports that he plays. All the guys love Larry because he is either friends with or knows every girl, which is why his parties are always the best.

As Jeremy is thinking about all of those guys, he replies to his father, "I know this decision should be really easy, but I kind of feel like I'd be abandoning those guys. I'm not saying this to sound cocky, but I think that they kind of look up to me a little because they all think I'm so good."

"It's good you feel that way, son. It shows that your mother and I raised you right. It shows that you have heart and compassion. But let's be honest for a second. Without you and Ricky, they really aren't a championship level team. I know you like those boys. Heck, I like a lot of those boys, but they are going to hold you back, not push you forward. It's time now for you to be a little selfish and do what's best for your future. It's not the time to worry about anyone but yourself, and don't forget, any decision you make now will impact your future."

"Mom, what do you think?"

"After listening to your father, I really have to agree with him. You need to do the best thing for you, Honey. I'll be happy with whatever decision you make, but I do think that you've worked really hard for these opportunities. Now that they are here, it seems silly not to take advantage of them." His mother turns her attention back to the stove and continues stirring the searing meat.

"All right, Buddy. Why don't you head up those stairs and take a shower. We can talk more about all of this at dinner. I have a few tests

38

I should correct now anyway." Jeremy begins to walk up the stairs as his father goes over to the refrigerator. David takes a soda out of the fridge and shuts the door. He twists off the cap and takes a long pull. "Can you believe he's even thinking about not going to St. Michaels? That would be just insane."

"David, he can do what he wants, but I am sure he will make the right decision." Jeremy's mother Jessica may not necessarily like to get involved in all of the sports talk, but she sure doesn't mind all of the dotting that comes along with it. As most mothers are, she is very proud of her son's accomplishments. But, what she really likes is the fact that everyone *knows* how good her boy is. Every other mom from the team is consistently going out of their way to talk to her or invite her and David over for coffee just to chat.

It's wasn't like she was unpopular growing up; quite the contrary in fact. She had played sports her whole life and had made many friends from it. Also, as soon as she hit the ninth grade and matured, the boys all noticed her as well. However, as life moved on and her friends either got married or moved away, more and more of her life became simply work and family. Not that she would ever complain, she had a very loving husband and a wonderful son in Jeremy. But if she wasn't at work, she was at one of Jeremy's practices or games. If she wasn't doing that, she was cleaning the house or cooking. Her social life revolved heavily around Jeremy's sports schedule.

Then this year something interesting began to happen. As it became clearer and clearer just how good her son really is and what he meant to the team, people started to want to talk to her more and more. It was as if her popularity grew right alongside his, and to be honest, she thought it was nice to engage in social adult interaction outside of work again. She would never let on, but she could already see Jeremy going to St. Michaels and her and David becoming the center of attention at every gala, dinner, and function that the school put on. Everyone would want to talk to them and shower the two with praise as to how they raised such a nice young man and how he was a star in the making.

Her husband's voice brings her back to the present, "I mean he just can't go to the local high school. That team's been bad for such a long time. He'll get so bogged down trying to do everything for that team that he will never really be able to grow to his full potential."

"I'm not saying I don't agree with you. We can make sure that we guide him to what we know is the best decision for him, but, ultimately, he has to make the final call. I don't want to be like those other parents that never let their kids make any decisions for themselves." David takes another long sip from his soda, "Can't you just see it now? Jeremy leads St. Michael's to straight championships and gets scholarship offers from every major Division I school in the country!"

He finishes his soda with one long gulp and places the bottle on the counter. "Let's not get too ahead of ourselves, dear. First, let's talk to him tonight and see where his heart is. Then we can make sure he has all the information he needs to make the right decision. Now, why don't you set the table and get ready to eat."

Jeremy finishes toweling off and wipes the condensation from the mirror. He stands there looking at himself and begins to think. Was he really going to leave behind all of his best friends? What would they say to him? Would they still be his friends if he went to St. Michael's? Would they think he was some sort of traitor? Deep down he knows what the real questions is: could he really pass up the opportunity to play at St. Michael's under Coach Fletcher and all of the things that would go along with that.

4

Ricky sprints up his front steps and slams through the door. "Dad!" His voice echoes throughout the entire house. He is so excited to tell his father about what had happened at the field that he can hardly control himself. "Dad, you home?" Ricky knows the answer to the question. Of course his father is home; he doesn't go anywhere anymore, just to the liquor store and back. He runs upstairs and continues calling for his father as he looks from room to room. "Dad!" He jogs back down the stairs and continues to call out.

A loud grumble comes up from the basement, "What are you yelling about, boy?" His father slowly moves his way up the stairs from the cellar, banging into both sides of the hallway as he does so. He reaches the top step, stumbles a little, and then slowly corrects his balance. "What the hell are you yelling about?"

It kills Ricky to see his father like this, but then again, he has gotten used to it. Years had passed as the man he once knew simply faded away. Ricky felt that, at times, his father forgot that two people lost something that night. Deep down he really thought that it was selfish of his father to simply quit on both of them the way that he has. Ricky also knows that thinking like this will get him nowhere. His father is drunk, again, like he is every other day.

"Dad, I got an offer to play at St. Michaels today from Coach Fletcher." His father breathes out audibly and staggers past Ricky to the refrigerator. He fumbles around in the fridge and grabs a can of beer. He rests his arm on top of the refrigerator door and cracks opens the can. Foam spills onto the floor as he raises the can to his lips and takes a very long sip, nearly finishing the can in one swig.

"Well, isn't that great for you." His father belches loudly and laughs a little. "That was a good one."

"Yeah, dad. That was a great one." Ricky does his best to hide his disappointment, but it can't help but show through in his words. "Don't you even care about what I'm telling you? Even just a little? I'm going to go to St. Michael's! This is what we always used to talk about."

Pain appears in his father's face, and his eyes begin to well with tears, "You know your mother and I really wanted you to go to that school. But, we weren't sure you'd be able to get in. She would have been really proud of you." His father finishes the beer, crushes the can, and throws it in the direction of the sink. He turns and grabs another beer out of the fridge, pops it open and takes another exceptionally long sip.

Suddenly, a wide grin spreads across his face, "Hey, we should celebrate. Here." His father tries to duck his head back into the fridge but strikes his forehead hard against the top of the opening of the door. He curses himself for being so clumsy and shakes it off. He reaches in and takes out another can of beer. He extends the can to his son. "You've earned it, son. Here, have a beer with your old man."

Ricky grasps the can in his hand and looks at it. It isn't like he's never had a beer before; his father has been giving him sips since he was a little boy. Also, every once in a while he would have one or two beers at one of Brett Rose's parties. He was able to get away with this because Brett's parents were usually out of town. But, thought Ricky, what father offers a beer to their 8th grade son as a show of celebration? He puts the beer down on the counter, "No thanks, Dad."

"Come on, what's the matter? Too good for a drink with your father?"

"I'm in the 8th grade. That's what's the matter."

"You finished 8th grade. You'll be in high school in a matter of months. I had my first beer as a sophomore. It's no big deal." His father takes another long drink and polishes off his second beer in a matter of minutes. He takes aim and launches the can towards the sink again. The can crashes into the sink, spinning and rolling around for a few moments before finally coming to rest at the base of the sink.

"Whatever, more for me then." He reaches out his hand and swipes the can off the counter. He snaps it open and takes in a mouthful. His father wobbles a bit but then steadies himself by placing his left hand on the counter. "So, you definitely going to accept and go to St. Michaels?"

"I don't think now is the best time to talk about this, Dad."

"What are you talking about? You were just running through the house shouting like a madman for me. Well, here I am. So, like I said,

44

you going to go there or what?" Ricky rolls his eyes and takes a seat at the kitchen table. "This is something I've wanted for a really long time. So, yes. I'm absolutely going to go there in the Fall. The coach gave me his card and wanted me to give it to you. He said if you had any questions to give him a call." Ricky fishes around in his pocket and pulls out the glossy business card. He takes a long look at it and then hands it to his father.

"Wow! This is fancy-looking. Look at how shiny it is." His father hiccups and takes another sip of his beer. "Well, maybe I'll call him. I want to know if you're going to play right away. I want to know what his plans are for my boy."

"Dad, please don't call him when you are like this."

"Like what? I'm just fine, thank you very much." He takes another long sip and finishes off yet another beer. "Man these things go down fast!"

"Dad, how many have you had today?"

"I don't know. It's not like I keep count or anything. Hey, check this out!" His father takes the can and places it on his forehead.

"What are you doing?"

"Just wait a second." He moves the can away from his head and slams it back into his forehead crushing the can completely. "Ha! How about that!"

"Wow, Dad. That was really great." Ricky says as sarcastically as he can. Ricky shakes his head and stands up from the table. "I'm going to go wash up and head over to Jeremy's house to eat."

"Hey, why don't you just eat here with me?"

"Because we don't have any food in this house, that's why." Ricky starts to make his way upstairs when his father calls out, "We can order pizza or something."

"Thanks for the offer, Dad, but I'd really like to have a nice home-cooked meal." Ricky's dad shrugs and walks over to the fridge. He pulls out three more cans of beer and staggers back down to the basement. He half falls, half sits, down on the couch and opens another beer.

He knows that he should be more excited for his son, that he should get sober and call that coach and talk to him about Ricky's future. He also knows all of the other things that he should do as opposed to what he is going to do, which is just drink the day away again like he has done all week.

It isn't like he hasn't tried to kick the booze before; it's just that he always ends up back in the same place that he starts off. The loss of his wife has proven to be too much for him to bear when he's clear-headed. Through the multiple tries to get sober, he has come to the realization that the only way he can deal with her passing is to get loaded every single day.

Since the accident, he really can't work; at least, not like he could before. He had been a foreman at a major construction company in the city. He was really good with his hands and had been exceptionally good at his job.

His father had been a carpenter, his grandfather had been a carpenter, and his uncles were all carpenters. So he had been around it his whole life. His boss loved him and promoted him to the highest position at the company, overseeing all of the projects that they were working on. After the accident, he really couldn't put much weight on one of his legs and just found excuse after excuse not to go back to work. Eventually, after a very long and arduous process, the settlement came in, and he no longer had any reason at all to return to the job he once loved.

Doug puts the drink to his lips and jerks his head back violently. Beer gushes down his throat, spilling down his chin and onto his shirt in the process. His bloodshot eyes fill with tears, and he begins to sob quietly. Water streams from his eyes and tears meander down his unshaven face until they eventually fall effortlessly to the ground below. He shakes his head from side to side and uses the bottom part of his shirt to wipe his face. He places the empty beer can on the ground and reaches for a second. As he does so, he thinks to himself that this is what his life has become.

He is now an absolute mess who just can't find the resolve to do anything, due to the loss of his beloved wife. He doesn't want to keep

47

letting his son down time and time again. It is just easier than dealing with the alternative. His wife is gone; that part of his life is over. He grabs the remote control for the television and presses the power button, and waits for it to take him away from his thoughts.

Ricky opens the door to his room and takes off his sweaty shirt. He balls it up and whips it into a corner. He hates seeing his father like this, especially because he remembers the man he used to be. Now, he is little more than a drunk. Ricky had hoped for some time that the father he once knew was still in there and would rise to the surface once again.

Years later, he now has very little hope that he will ever see that man again. He grabs a duffel bag that is sitting in the corner of his closet and begins to stuff it with clothes. He takes the bag into the bathroom and tosses in some deodorant, his toothbrush, toothpaste, and some hair gel. He goes back into his room and throws on a new T-shirt. He doesn't want to be in this house anymore today. He can just shower at Jeremy's house when he gets there.

He flies down the steps and yells in the direction of the basement, "I'm going to Jeremy's house. I'm probably just going to sleep there tonight." He waits for his father's response but hears nothing. He quietly walks down the steps leading to the basement. His father is there, lying on the couch with the television on. Three crumpled up beer cans lie feebly on the floor in front of him. Ricky can hear his father snoring ever-so-slightly and feels a wretch of pain in his

48

gut. His father is a broken man. A single tear rolls down his right cheek, which he quickly swipes away with the shoulder of his T-shirt. He puts a hand on his father's shoulder, "I still love you, Dad" and walks back up the stairs.

The truth is, Ricky knows his father loves him very much. He just isn't able to find his way to that place in his heart right now. Maybe he never will again, at least, not the same way as before when they were a whole family. Ricky shoulders his duffel bag and walks towards the front door. He opens the door and steps out into the gleaming sunshine. The warmth of the sun quickly dries the wetness leftover on his cheeks from his wiped away tears. He hikes the bag up a little higher onto his shoulder and begins the walk to Jeremy's house.

The doorbell resonates loudly throughout the house. David looks up from his test papers, "Hey Jess, can you get that?"

"I'm a little busy right now making supper. How about you get it since you're closer." David huffs to himself as he gets up. He makes his way over to the front door. He grasps the handle and opens the door to reveal a puffy-eyed Ricky standing before him. Ricky sniffles a little, "Hi, Mr. Savage. Mind if I come in?"

"Of course not, Ricky. Jess said you'd probably be stopping by. Is everything ok?"

Ricky nods and closes the door behind him. "Yeah, I'm ok. It's just my dad, you know. I was kind of excited to tell him about St. Michael's, but he's been drinking again, as usual. I don't know why I thought today would be any different." Ricky continues, "You know he offered me a can of beer to celebrate? Who does that to their eighth-grade son?"

"Oh honey, I'm so sorry." Jessica walks over to Ricky and gives him a big hug. After Ricky's mom passed, Jessica sort of took the role over. She never tries to lecture him, but she is always there if he needs to talk. His father's never really in any shape to have an actual conversation, plus, for some reason, Ricky just feels a little more comfortable talking to her than anyone else about certain things.

Perhaps it is because he's known her his whole life or maybe it's just her way, but she has this knack for being able to make him feel better about whatever is bothering him. Although he and Jeremy are these tough football players and great athletes, they are still just kids and sometimes, it's is nice to let the guard down a little bit.

Jeremy shouts from his room, "Hey, I heard the doorbell. Is that you, Ricky?"

"Yeah, it's me. Hurry up and get down here! I'm starving!" Ricky smiles at Jessica and quietly thanks her. David puts his hand on Ricky's head and ruffles his hair, "You know that you're welcome here anytime, Ricky, really. If you ever need anything, don't hesitate to ask us."

David and Jessica know it's no use to try and talk with Ricky's dad, Doug. They have tried countless times over the last few years, but nothing ever got through to him. So now, they do what they think is best: they take care of Ricky and look after him as if he is their own.

A few moments later, Jeremy bounds down the steps and comes to a stop just before crashing into Ricky, "So, did you talk to your dad? What'd he say? Was he excited for you?" Ricky looks from David's face to Jessica's, "Yeah, he was happy for me. He thinks that I should definitely go to St. Michael's."

Jeremy's mother pipes in, "Hey, let's sit and eat before the food gets cold?"

"That's a great idea, Dear. Let's eat."

51

The four of them walk into the kitchen and take their seats at the dinner table. Jeremy barely wastes any time chewing as he consumes his pasta and meatballs at a furious rate. "Jeez, slow down! It's not like your food is going to run away or anything," says Ricky.

Jeremy takes a huge gulp of water and laughs a bit, "Yeah, but after all that practice today, I'm starving."

David finishes off a meatball and puts his fork down, "You know, you two should be very proud of yourselves. It took a lot of hard work and commitment on both your parts to be where you are right now. Ricky, I couldn't help but overhear you when you were talking to Jeremy. It seems like you already have made up your mind about going to St. Michael's."

"Yeah, for me it was never really a question. I've always wanted to go there if I was able to play. I just thank the stars for these golden hands every day!"

"I think I'm going to throw up, golden hands. You should be thanking me for throwing to you so much."

"Ha! As if you have a better option. You're just going to have to face it, my friend; my hands are like magnets to footballs."

"Let it never be said that Ricky Goodman lacks confidence!" exclaims Jeremy.

Everyone laughs and continues eating. Through the laughter, Ricky's mood begins to lighten up. He looks at the three faces surrounding him at the dinner table and feels so lucky to have each of them in his life.

The fun and conversation continue on for another fifteen minutes or so before Jeremy's mom begins to point out all of the great things that St. Michael's has to offer.

"You know, boys. St. Michael's has an excellent reputation for education as well as state of the art facilities. You'll not only be able to expand your skills on the field, but also get the best education available to you. Also, I kind of like the idea of seeing you two in uniforms. It will make you look so grown up!"

"Uniforms. Not exactly something I'm looking forward to." Ricky continues, "But I guess it's not the worst thing in the world. At least I know what I'm going to wear every day."   Jeremy reaches up from his seat to grab a roll and some butter. He slathers butter all over the roll and jams an oversized piece into his mouth. "I don't think uniforms would bother me all that much. I'm sure you get used to it pretty fast."

The dinner conversation continues on for a little while longer with Jeremy's mother highlighting all of the positives of St. Michael's. When dinner is over, Ricky and Jeremy help clean off the table. "That was really good, Mrs. Savage. Thanks again for dinner," said Ricky.

"You're very welcome, Ricky."

"Hey, Ricky. Want to go play some videogames?"

"Sounds good to me, but get ready to get your butt kicked."

"We didn't even decide what game to play yet."

Ricky starts to run up the stairs, "As if that matters! I beat you in every game."

The two sprint up the stairs to Jeremy's room and burst through the door.

Jeremy's room looks very much like any teenage boys' room might, with one exception. It is painted a deep shade of blue and has white moldings around the doors and windows. His walls are littered with photos and posters of all of his favorite football players and cars. Over his bed is a giant picture of his favorite player in the middle of his throwing motion.

To the left and right of the player are the helmets of the local professional team. On the far wall he has a photo or poster of every dream car imaginable: Porsche, Ferrari, Lamborghini, and Corvette are all well-represented.

The possessions located on the wall opposite the cars are what make Jeremy's room a little different. His father installed a small white shelf when Jeremy was just a little boy to put his trophies on. However, Jeremy quickly needed another, and another, and another. Now, the wall has eight shelves crammed full of trophies in varying sizes, along with medals, plaques, and framed certificates.

As a result of all of his athletic accomplishments, Jeremy has already managed to amass more hardware than all of the other kids in the town put together; pretty impressive for only being in the eighth grade! Jeremy's dad often jokes with him that soon his trophies will require their own room, forcing Jeremy to go and sleep in the guest room.

Also located in Jeremy's room is a modest desk in one corner, which he uses to do his homework. Sitting on top of the desk is a laptop which Jeremy uses regularly. Resting on the floor is one of his most prized-possessions: his game chair. He had asked his parents for one this past year, and there it was on Christmas morning. The chair has a full set of four built-in speakers designed to really enhance the gaming experience. It also rocks back and forth which Jeremy really likes.

"Alright, I don't know about you, but I'm feeling like some football. You in?"

Ricky nods, "Sounds good to me."

Jeremy walks over to the game system and pops open a disc. He slides the disc into the game system and grabs two controllers off the shelf. "You want the red one or the blue one?"

"I'll take red," says Ricky.

Jeremy tosses the controller to Ricky, who snatches it out of the air with one hand. "See that? Like I said, I can catch anything!"

Ricky struts over to the gaming chair and sits down in it laughing. Jeremy shakes his head and turns on his controller. "Hey, I got some good news today."

"Duh, I know. I was there."

"No, not that. I mean, that was good news too. I got invited to the football camp I really wanted to go to out in California. It's in a few weeks."

"Good for you! That's pretty cool. Wait a minute. In a few weeks? We need to keep practicing if we are going to play right away at St. Michael's. How long is the camp?"

Jeremy selects the team he wants to use for the game, "It's only for a week, and I told you I'm not sure I want to go to St. Michael's."

Ricky scoffs, "Are you seriously going to use that team against me? Like I said before, butt… kicking. Anyway, I guess a week is no biggie. I can just do some extra work on my speed and training for a while. The bigger problem is where will I eat dinner for a week without you around?"

The game starts, and Ricky takes the opening kickoff all the way for a touchdown. "Ha ha! I told you I'm going to crush you!"

"How does that even happen? It's like my team is just running around like a bunch of dummies not trying to tackle your guys. It's ridiculous!"

"Listen, buddy. Don't be sad. It's ok. Look, I promise that I'll take it easy on you if it gets really bad." Ricky laughs loudly and moves his thumbs around on the control stick smashing his defensive end into Jeremy's quarterback, causing him to fumble.

"OOHHH YEEAH!! I'll take the football, thank you very much. That looks like it really hurt. Hopefully that never happens to you in one of our games!"

Jeremy shakes the controller vigorously as he watches Ricky's defender pick up the football and take it another twenty yards downfield before being tackled. Jeremy stands up from his seat and begins shouting at the television, "Yeah right, like that happens all the time or something! Seriously, in this stupid game this guy fumbles every single time! If he did that in real life, he'd never be on a team!"

Ricky can't help but laugh at Jeremy. Every time they play a game together, Jeremy goes wild about something. It is really funny to Ricky because Jeremy is always so calm about everything else. However, when he starts losing in a videogame or one of his guys does something stupid, off he goes, and this time is no exception.

Jeremy sits there muttering under his breath as Ricky's quarterback pitches the ball to his running back. He then proceeds to run over and around every single one of Jeremy's defenders easily taking it all the way "to the house." Jeremy shoots up out of his chair again.

"You've got to be kidding me! Did you see that? Every guy on my team sucks. Not one of them can tackle a pee-wee football player! Absolutely pathetic!"

The game continues in this fashion with Jeremy getting a few good plays in on his way to a very bad 56-21 loss.

"You know we are playing again, right?" says Jeremy.

"Are you sure you can handle getting stomped on again?"

A look of determination settles over Jeremy's face, "Here we go! New teams this time. Those guys are awful."

Three more victories later, Ricky gets up from his chair and dusts off his shoulders, "Well, that was a little embarrassing for you my friend." He stretches out and takes a look at the clock. "Hey, it's a little late. Do you think your parents would mind if I just stayed over tonight?"

"I don't think they care, but hold on a second."

Jeremy walks over to his doorway and yells down the stairs, "Mom!"

"What is it, Jeremy?"

"Do you and Dad care if Ricky sleeps over?"

Jessica looks over her coffee in the direction of her husband who is still busily correcting papers. "David, you don't mind do you?"

"Mind what?"

"If Ricky stays over."

"Of course not."

"It's ok with us if it's ok with Ricky's dad!" She yells up the stairs.

"Ok, thanks!" He turns to Ricky, "They said they don't care as long as…" Jeremy stops in the middle of his sentence because Ricky

58

has put his hands up. "I'm right here, I can hear them. Yeah, it's ok with my dad. I told him I was probably going to stay here when I left."

"Well, now that's settled, how about we play one more game?"

Ricky picks up the controller, "Hey, I enjoy winning, so as far as I'm concerned, we can play this game all night if you want."

Ricky wouldn't let on to his friend, but he is really thankful that he has Jeremy and Jeremy's parents in his life. With them, he can come and get his mind off of the things that are going on at home. He also really likes being around a normal family and doing all of the things that normal families do. Without them, he isn't really sure what he would be doing with himself, outside of football. He knows one thing for sure; he wouldn't be at home.

Ricky takes off his socks, balls them up, and tosses them in the corner. He makes a few movements with his thumbs and selects the next team he's going to use. Jeremy cracks his knuckles, "Alright, I'm ready this time. Those other games were just warm-ups."

"Whatever you say Savvy. Get ready to get lit up like a Christmas tree!"

"Hey Ricky, since you're staying over, do you want to come to Zach's house with me in the morning?

"Let me guess. You and Meathead are going to go to the gym together?"

Ricky likes Zach, but still enjoys poking fun at him from time-to-time.

59

"Why don't you call him a meathead to his face? He'll probably stuff you in a trash can!" Jeremy starts cracking up laughing and slaps his knee. "I can picture your feet sticking straight up out of the can trying desperately to get out, calling for help, but no one comes to help you. That would be hilarious!"

"Yeah, very funny Buddy, very funny. Just keep laughing. Let's see if you're laughing after I demolish you in football for the hundredth time." Ricky continues, "If we are going to see Zach, is Walter going to be there too?"

"I think so, but Zach didn't say anything when I talked to him earlier." Jeremy pulls his cell phone out of his pocket, "I'll text him real quick and ask him." Jeremy punches some buttons on the phone with blistering speed and hits send. A second later, his phone vibrates, "Zach says that Walter's there right now and plans on sleeping over, so, yeah, he'll still be there by the time we get there in the morning. Want me to call him a meathead for you?'

Jeremy laughs and sends another message to Zach informing him that he and Ricky will meet them in the morning at his house. Ricky pretends like he is juking defenders in his seat as he controls one of his players,

"Uh oh! He's at the thirty, the twenty, the ten, touchdown! This is just too easy, too easy, I say."

Jeremy kicks his foot out in frustration, "Maybe I'm really just not as good at this game as I think I am. I mean, I always beat the computer."

Ricky looks at his friend and jokes, "Dude, everybody always beats the computer. If you want to find out if you're any good, you've got to play against other people online, or you can play against me and get crushed, it's up to you."

Jeremy and Ricky continue to battle well into the night until their eyes eventually close and sleep gets the better of them.

6

Jeremy, Ricky, Walter, and Zach have been working out at the gym for the past hour, although, if you looked at Walter, you would have thought it had been more like six hours. The guy is completely drenched in sweat. Suddenly, the phone in Jeremy's pocket begins to vibrate. He takes it out and looks at it. It is a text message from Brett Rose. "Hey guys, want to go to a party at Brett's tonight?" Jeremy scrolls down to read the rest of the group messages, "Jeff's going. So are Jake and Larry and some other guys from the team."

At this, Zach's ears perk up, "If Larry's going, girls will be there, which means I will be there."

Jeremy continues, "Yeah, Larry's going. It also looks like Brett's parents are out of town and we can all sleep there if we want."

Zach flexes his muscles, which are inflated more than usual due to the workout, "Pool party; love it! It will give me a chance to show off the pipes I've spent all day sculpting."

Ricky laughs and gives Zach a light shove.

Walter says, "Well, no one's ever home at my house, so I'm in."

Ricky looks at Jeremy, "You know I'm in. I hate sleeping at home. Are you going to go?" Jeremy pauses for a moment, "I'm not sure my parents will let me go if Brett's parents aren't home, but I'll ask them when I get home."

"We can all pretend like we are going to sleep at my house. Jeremy, your mom can even call and talk to my mom" says Zach. "Later on, I'll tell my mom that we changed our minds and we are going to go to Brett's house and sleep there instead. My mom never calls if I tell her I'm sleeping out. She'll be happy that I'm not there eating everything or making a racket."

Ricky agrees, "Terminator here is right. Have your mom call Zach's mom. Later, we can all go to Brett's and enjoy the party."

Jeremy doesn't like the idea of lying to his parents, but he knows that he can't miss one of Brett's famous parties either, so he agrees to the plan.

That evening, Jeremy and Ricky inhale their dinners, quickly clean off their plates and place them into the dishwasher. "Mom, do you mind if I sleep over Zach's tonight? Ricky and Walter are going too. We are all going to play this new game that Walter bought. You can call Zach's mom if you want. She said that she'd be home if you wanted to check-in with her."

Jeremy's mother looks to her husband who just shrugs. "I'll call Zach's mom and make sure she is ok with it. If she is, then it's fine with us."

"Great!" Jeremy flies up the stairs and packs a bag, making sure to put in some of his nicest looking clothes for the party. He just got a new T-shirt he really likes, and he decides that this is the perfect opportunity to break it out. He tosses in some khaki shorts as well as

63

some other stuff to sleep in. He slings the bag over his shoulder and looks at Ricky, "Ready to go?"

"Aren't you forgetting some stuff? Like toothpaste, deodorant…"

Jeremy puts up a hand indicating for Ricky to stop and heads into the bathroom. He takes a few things and puts them into a large plastic bag so that they will not dirty up his shirt and shorts for the night. He sticks his head into the bedroom opening, "Ready?" Ricky leaps up off the chair, shoulders his own bag, and heads out of the room.

Jeremy and Ricky reach the bottom of the stairs just as Jeremy's mother is hanging up the phone. She looks towards the boys, "I just got off the phone with Zach's mother, and she said it was fine if you two slept over. Jeremy, don't make too much noise there. You know how you are when you play videogames. Ricky, did you run this by your father?"

"Yeah, I told him I was going to eat here and then sleep at Zach's, not that he'd even notice." Jessica sighs and looks away. It pains her deeply that Ricky's father is wasting away in front of her eyes and that there is nothing she or David can do about it. "Have fun boys, but be respectful of their house, just like you do whenever you are here. I'll see you both in the morning, I'm assuming?"

"Yeah, I've got to grab some clothes and my cleats before I head to summer drills," replies Jeremy.

64

"I'll probably be with him," said Ricky. With that, the two shoot out of the front door and walk at a very quick pace towards Zach's.

By the time Jeremy and Ricky get to the house, Zach is already ready to go. He is wearing a new, tightly-fitting, cut-off T-shirt, which highlights his well-toned physique. Ricky scoffs, "Dude, don't you think you're trying a little too hard with that shirt? Maybe you should just wear a regular T-shirt and not one that looks like it was made for an eight year-old."

Zach checks himself out in a mirror, "Are you kidding? Why do you think I lift all those weights? Part of it is for football, but the other part is to show off! Besides, this is a large shirt. It's not my fault that my muscles simply can't be contained by any shirt."

Jeremy laughs, "Hey, you mind if I change in your bathroom?"

"No. Why would I mind if you use my bathroom, weirdo?"

"I'm just asking." Jeremy picks up his bag and strides into the bathroom to change. A few minutes later, Jeremy comes out of the bathroom and walks into Zach's room. "Hey, where's Walter?"

Zach responds, "He's going to meet us at Brett's. He's playing that game he just got online and is apparently destroying everyone. So, he's going to keep playing for a bit and then meet us later."

Ricky checks himself out in the mirror one final time, "You boys ready to have some fun?"

Zach double-checks his hair, "I know I'm ready."

Jeremy straightens out his T-shirt one last time, "Me too."

65

"Then let's get to it!"

Zach is followed closely by Jeremy and Ricky as he walks down the stairs. Zach calls out to his mother, "Mom!"

A response from a different room can barely be heard. "What is it Zach?"

"We decided to go to Brett's tonight instead. He's ordering pizza, and we are going to watch a movie."

"Ok, have fun." Zach turns to look back at the others, "What did I tell you? Foolproof plan! Do you guys want to walk or get a ride?"

Brett's house is about a twenty-minute walk from Zach's, but it is a really nice night, so the three decide that the walk would be fine. As they walk from Zach's house to Brett's, they take turns busting each other up along the way about everything from the clothes they are wearing to the past football season.

They arrive and strut up Brett's driveway, cracking up laughing from all of the jokes. Zach knocks on the front door. No answer. The music inside is audible from the front stairs which could be the reason why no one comes to the door. Jeremy looks at Zach, "Think we should just walk in?"

Zach ponders this for only a moment and grabs at the door handle. He thrusts the door open and reveals the bustling party taking place within. Zach smiles instantly. This is his kind of scene.

The lights are turned down low, and the music is playing loudly as they walk through the door. There are kids from their football team present, as well as a bunch of other kids from the high school, some much older than Brett. Those kids are friends with his sister, Nicole, who is going to be a senior this year.

To be honest, it's really her party. She is just allowing her brother to invite some of his friends so that he won't tell on her when their parents came back home from vacation.

Many of the older kids have red cups in their hands, which Jeremy figures must have some sort of alcohol in it. He sheepishly looks at Ricky, feeling a little guilty for having deceived his mother and being around this sort of thing. He knows better than to be caught up in stuff like this. His best friend, knowing him the way that he does, is able to determine exactly what Jeremy is thinking, "Savvy, everything is going to be fine. She's never going to find out we're here."

Ricky's words reassure Jeremy very little. Ricky continues, "Besides, do you really want to miss all this?" Ricky extends a hand towards the sights and sounds before them and motions from side to side, making sure that Jeremy takes in the full experience.

Jeremy smiles a bit, "I guess you're right."

"Of course I'm right! Now let's try to have a good time. Why don't we see if we can find some of the guys?"

Larry is standing in the back corner of the living room. He looks as suave as ever with a massive group of girls encircling him. He is talking about some sort of audition he attended, for a short film that is going to be taping in the fall. Naturally, all of the girls are eating that up. Jeremy and Ricky walk up to Larry, "What's up, Larry?"

"Hey, what up, Ricky? Savvy, my man. How's it going? I've got to say I'm happy to see you two here. Ladies, if you don't already know, these are my friends Ricky and Jeremy. Jeremy here is going to be the next best thing to come out of Centerville. You may want to grab onto this guy now before he's too hot to touch. Ricky here is the fastest thing I've ever seen on two feet, a lock to start varsity this year as a freshman."

One of the girls turns and faces Jeremy. Jeremy knows exactly who she is. Lauren Wilkins is going to be a sophomore at Centerville High this year. She lives only a few streets over from him. Jeremy sees her from time-to-time hanging around the neighborhood with her friends or at some of her little brothers' football games. Her brother is two years younger than Jeremy, so her brothers' team plays after Jeremy's. Jeremy loves football, both playing and watching, he often sticks around to watch the younger kids play after his game is finished. He has seen Lauren a number of times while watching those games.

Lauren has flawless skin, deep brown eyes and shiny brown hair. She has a perfect smile, and little dimples that can be seen when she laughs. From the first time he saw her, Jeremy has always thought that she is the most beautiful thing he has ever seen. Seeing her tonight, he can't help but stare at her. She smiles at him and begins to talk, but Jeremy can't really hear anything she says because of the music. He is

68

also way too enamored with her beauty to actually be paying attention to her words. He tries to focus while she is talking, but is really just staring at her lips moving, not caring what words are coming out of them.

Apparently, she is asking him a question. When he doesn't answer, she repeats it. Jeremy, still hearing nothing, finding himself completely unable to focus on anything but her face.

A sharp pain in his ribs breaks his trance. Ricky's jab achieves the desired effect.

"I'm sorry, what did you say? It's kind of loud in here."

Lauren smiles at Jeremy, highlighting her beautiful dimples. She tucks a strand of brown hair behind her ear, "I said, are you excited to be playing varsity next year?" Jeremy immediately feels hot. He still hasn't made up his mind about what school he is going to go to next year, but he really didn't want his friends, or anyone else, to find out that he may not be going to Centerville. He stammers, "Umm, well, I mean, I'm just excited to play at a different level next year. You know, looking forward to a new challenge."

"Yeah well, you've been pretty good over the years. Hopefully that can continue and you can lead Centerville to a state title."

Jeremy just nods and looks away from her, trying to avoid further conversation about Centerville High. "So, Lauren, how's your brother doing?" Even as he asks the question, he knows it sounds kind

69

of stupid, but he can't stop himself from asking it. It is like his brain is shut off, and he's just cruising on auto-pilot.

She replies, "Well, he's ok. You know, he really looks up to you. Winning the first championship in junior league history is a big deal to the younger guys."

Larry, who has his arms around two different girls, sees that his friend is struggling and interjects, "Lauren, you know, Jeremy is going to get a full ride to play at some big time Division I school one day. After that, who knows, maybe all the way to the pros."

Jeremy blushes a bit at the compliment his friend is paying him, but is also very thankful for the disruption. Lauren takes one of her arms and loops it around Jeremy's, "Maybe if I'm lucky, he'll take me with him."

Jeremy looks down and can feel his pulse quicken. She is actually touching his arm. Lauren Wilkins has her arm wrapped around his, on purpose. He smirks.

As the conversation continues, three more of the girls surround Ricky, Jeremy, and Lauren, all seemingly interested in the star quarterback.

One of the girls, Amanda Carrey, takes a step forward and places her hand on Jeremy's shoulder. "So, you're the one everyone's always talking about. Nice to finally meet you. I'm Amanda."

Jeremy, feeling a little uncomfortable with all the attention, shies away and barely ekes out a meek, "Hello".

Lauren looks at Amanda and gives her a disgusted look, "Hey Amanda. Jeremy and I are going to take a walk. Why don't you go and find your boyfriend?" Amanda, sensing Lauren's irritation, backs away and fades into the crowd.

What Jeremy does not know is that as much as he likes Lauren, she has felt the same way about him for some time. She just never really had the chance to tell him; at least, not until tonight. She has always thought Jeremy was pretty cute, just about every girl does. But what had really gotten to her was something that happened about a year ago. Lauren and her parents were at the practice field watching her brother's team scrimmage a team from Oakville. After the game, her brother remained on the field working on running some routes that he had messed up during the game. Jeremy noticed what he was doing and went over to help. He stayed on the field with him for at least an hour or so, working on route running. He wasn't looking for anything in return; he was just a really nice kid helping out her little brother. Lauren feels that Jeremy is a great guy that all the younger kids adore because he is incredibly talented, yet extremely humble. After that day, she saw him in a new light. She knew that he was something more than just some jock who could throw a ball better than everyone else, and tonight she was determined to let him know how she felt.

Lauren leans in close to Jeremy and asks, "Do you mind if we go for a walk?" Jeremy's mind begins to race. What did she want? Did he do something wrong? He begins to sweat a little and feels the palms

71

of his hands getting clammy. He looks to Ricky, who is just standing there grinning at him.

Being Jeremy's best friend, he knows exactly how Jeremy feels about Lauren. He also knows that, although Jeremy is as confident as can be on the football field, he is the exact opposite with girls. If Lauren hadn't come up to him, he probably would not have had the guts to talk to her all night.

Jeremy splutters out an, "ok" and the two walk towards the front door. On the way out, Larry gives Jeremy a quick slap on the back. Jeremy quickly turns his head and sees Larry winking at him as Lauren leads him out the door. Larry then turns and looks from one of his girls to the other, "I think we should head towards the pool. What do you ladies think?"

The two girls giggle in agreement, and the three of them walk towards the back of the house towards the pool.

In the corner of the living room sits a boy not talking to anyone. He is wrenching his hands and has a deep scowl on his face. He is not enjoying the music, he is not drinking anything, he is simply sitting alone. He appears as out of place as a person can be at a party. As Jeremy and Lauren walk past him, he simply stares in disbelief. How could she pick this kid? What did that guy have that he didn't? As he continues to think about these things, rage forms inside of him. He lashes out and strikes a nearby end table. The table crumbles under the force of his blow. No one hears the destruction; no one even looks in his direction. As he watches his ex-girlfriend walk out of the front door with some punk kid, he can't help but feel betrayed.

They had only broken up a year ago. How can she already be looking to move on? He had tried to get back together with her time and time again, but nothing he did seemed to work. The more he thinks about it, the angrier he becomes. He stands up quietly, storms towards the front door, and bumps hard into a girl along the way. He doesn't acknowledge the girl at all and continues right out the door, shutting it behind him as he exits.

Nicole's shoulder jerks back hard as someone moving very quickly slams into her. As she is about to tell the person to watch out or they could leave her party, the person is gone just as abruptly as he had arrived. She is able to see the boy's face as he thunders through the crowd and exits the house. Immediately, Nicole looks from side to side, as if she is searching for something. She runs up to one of her friends, "Sarah, have you seen Lauren? Do you know where she is?" Sarah shakes her head no, "I haven't seen her in a little bit. She was talking to Larry last time I saw her." Nicole rushes past Sarah and bursts into the kitchen looking for either her brother or Larry. Brett is sitting at the kitchen table talking to Jeff and Jake. She runs up to him, "Have you seen Larry?"

"Yeah, he just went outside to the pool with a couple of girls. Why?" Nicole, having no time to waste, rushes through the screen door leading to the backyard and heads straight for the pool. Larry is in the

73

pool frolicking in the water with the two girls. "Larry, have you seen Lauren?" Larry shakes the water from his head and brushes his soggy hair to the side. "Yeah, a little while ago. Why?"

"Where is she?"

Larry dunks himself back under the water and bounces up quickly. "She went for a walk with Jeremy."

Nicole freezes. "Did they go out the front?"

Larry nods his head yes. "Why?"

A chill runs up Nicole's spine.

Nathan Peters had always seemed like an average high school kid. He and Lauren dated for a long time, and Nicole had hung out with them on a number of occasions. To Nicole, Nathan seemed like a really nice guy until one day, Lauren abruptly ended their relationship. Nathan was absolutely devastated. He tried everything to get her back: flowers, apologies, gifts, everything. Nicole couldn't understand why Lauren had all-of-a-sudden broken up with Nathan. It took Nicole a long time to finally get Lauren to tell her what really happened.

Lauren told Nicole that Nathan was completely obsessed with her. He called and texted her all the time, and it got to the point where she couldn't do anything without him pestering her.

One night, Lauren decided to go out with her friends. She left her phone at home because she didn't want Nathan to bother her all night, like he did every other night. When she got home, Nathan was waiting for her in her bedroom. Her parents had been away for the weekend with her brother and allowed her to stay at home alone as long as she checked in every night before bed. He grabbed her when she came in and shoved her forcefully. She bounced off the bed and fell hard to the floor. He tried to apologize, but she shrieked for him to leave. He pleaded for her to listen to him and allow him to apologize for what he had done. Lauren began to scream at the top of her lungs, and he ran out the door. Ever since that day, Lauren knew that she couldn't trust Nathan. He had shown that there was a side of him that he kept hidden in the shadows.

Nicole had seen the look on his face as he walked out the front door. It was of blind fury, as if he simply was not able to control himself.

"Get out of the pool, Larry. We need to find Jeremy and Lauren, now!" The urgency in Nicole's voice prompts him to hurriedly get out of the water. Larry tries to grab a towel, but Nicole protests, "We don't have time for that. Where's Zach? We are going to need him."

Larry looks to his left and sees that Zach is there, flexing his muscles for a group of girls.

Nicole barrels through the group of females, "Zach, we need to go, now!" Zach asks no questions; he simply follows her and Larry as they run through the party and out the front door. Nicole races to the sidewalk and looks from left to right. In the distance, she can hear a girl sobbing. Zach strains to hear, "What is that?" Nicole whips around to face him, "I think someone is hurting Lauren and Jeremy."

A stony look forms over Zach's face. Larry bursts into a full sprint, having been able to determine the direction of the sounds. Zach and Nicole run after him. When they arrive, Nathan has his knees on Jeremy's shoulders and is pinning him down on the ground. He is screaming in Jeremy's face, "You think you're better than me? You think you can treat her better than I can?" Nathan balls up a fist and sends it plunging towards Jeremy's face.

Seeing this, Zach races at Nathan. Without even a hint of hesitation, Zach sends his body hurtling through the air and slams into Nathan before his punch connects with Jeremy.

The force of Zach's blast knocks Nathan clean off Jeremy and slams him hard to the ground. Zach tucks, rolls, and pops right back to his feet. He storms over to Nathan and grips his shirt hard. He lifts him to his feet and then heaves him off of them. Zach takes a step forward and shoves hard, simultaneously releasing his hold of Nathan. The push sends Nathan flying backwards through the air.

Nathan crashes to the ground, striking his backside hard on the unrelenting pavement. Zach jumps on top of Nathan and punches him hard in the face. "If you ever touch one of my friends again, I'll end you. Do you understand me?" Zach looks over his shoulder in the direction of Lauren, who is still sobbing. He then looks back to Nathan. "That goes for her too. If I hear you've even looked at either one of them funny, you'll deal with me. Understand?" Nathan moves his head up and down. "I don't think I heard you. Do you understand me or do I need to..?" Before he was able to get out another word, Nathan yells loudly, "I understand! I do! I won't even look at them. I promise." Zach gets up off Nathan and dusts off his shirt. "Now get out of here, before I get really mad."

Nathan jumps to his feet and disappears into the awaiting night.

Zach can see that Larry is helping Jeremy to his feet while Nicole is attempting to console Lauren. "Hey Jer, you all right?" Jeremy wipes the backside of his hand across his nose and notices it is bleeding a little. "Yeah, thanks. I owe you one."

"Please. I'd do anything for you guys. You're like my family."

Jeremy feels a pit in the bottom of his stomach. How is he ever going to tell Zach that he is thinking about leaving him next year?

As soon as Lauren sees that Jeremy is on his feet, she brakes free of Nicole's embrace and streaks towards him. "I'm so sorry, Jeremy! Nathan's crazy. We haven't been dating for over a year, I don't know what's wrong with him."

Jeremy, still a little foggy from the attack, smiles weakly. "Lauren it's ok, really, I don't blame you at all. It's not like this is all-of-a-sudden going to change the way I feel about you or anything. I've liked you forever."

As the words fall out of Jeremy's mouth, everyone goes completely silent. This is the first time any of them have ever heard Jeremy tell a girl that he likes her to her face. Lauren smiles brightly through her tears, "Good, because I really like you too." She thrusts her arms around Jeremy and grips him tightly, burying her face in his chest as she does so.

Larry is shaking his head in disbelief. "I can't believe you manhandled that kid like that. You literally lifted him off his feet and tossed him like a ragdoll. It was pretty epic. What the heck have you been taking lately?" asks Larry.

"All protein and hard work buddy," replies Zach. Then Zach announces, "Well, now that this whole deal is taken care of, how about we get back to the fun zone?"

Nicole agrees, "Yeah, we should get back and get some ice for your face, Jeremy. I don't want you to end up with two black eyes for practice tomorrow."

The group heads back to the party while Larry continues to reenact the fight along the walk.

7

When the four arrive back at the house, it is as if nothing has even happened. The party is still in full effect; the music is pumping, and loud laughter echoes throughout the house. Nicole walks Jeremy to the kitchen and takes out a bag of frozen peas, "Follow me upstairs."

She leads Jeremy upstairs to Brett's room. "I figured that you would prefer to do this in private."

"Thanks, I appreciate that."

"Here, put this on your face. It's going to be cold and might sting a little, but you're going to have to deal with it. Also, keep your chin pointed downward towards your chest to make sure the bleeding has totally stopped. I'll go tell Lauren that you're in here. I'm sure she'll want to see you."

Jeremy thanks her again as she closes the door on her way downstairs. He sits there alone in the darkness, pressing a bag of frozen peas to his injured nose and eye. Now that things have calmed down, he can finally take a moment to reflect on what transpired over the last hour.

He was on a walk with the girl of his dreams, trying feebly to hide his excitement. They rounded a corner, and out of the darkness came a crushing blow to the side of his head. The next thing he knew, his head was spinning and something heavy was holding him to the ground. He heard muffled sounds mixed with an unfamiliar voice yelling in his direction, but he couldn't make out any of the words. He wasn't sure if that was due to the blow to the head or something else. There was another stab of pain as something struck his face hard, dead in the center. He had felt warm liquid trickle out of his nose and down the side of his cheek. He was completely disoriented at his point, but then he suddenly felt the weight lift off of his body and someone or something was trying to lift him to his feet. A little while later, here he is, sitting on his friend's bed, nursing injuries.

There came an easy knock on the bedroom door. "Jeremy, is it ok if I come in?" Lauren's soft voice eases its way through the space between them.

"Yeah, come on in."

She opens the door just enough for her slender body to enter and closes it quickly behind her. She looks at him, pangs of guilt rack through her entire body. Although she knows it wasn't entirely her fault, it was still her psycho ex-boyfriend that did this to Jeremy. Because of that, there is a part of her that can't help but feel a little responsible. She sits down quietly next to him, gently removes the bag of peas and lifts his face so she can see. "Here, let me take a look." It doesn't appear as bad as she thought it would, but he will probably have a black eye or two tomorrow morning. "I can't believe he hit you like that."

"I never even saw it coming. Before I knew it, I was on the ground getting punched." Jeremy shifts his position on the bed and leans back, trying to make himself more comfortable. Lauren moves her focus from his face to the ceiling. She nervously fiddles with her fingers and tries to think of how she is going to say this. "Look, Jeremy, now that you've had a moment to think, I totally understand if you feel like some of this is my fault. I just want you to know how sorry I am that this happened."

Jeremy smiles and adjusts the bag of peas, "I don't blame you. How could I? You're not responsible for what other people do any more than I am. I'm not saying I'm thrilled I got punched in the face, but if I lost someone like you, I might go a little crazy too."

That was enough for her. She places her hands on either side of his face and gives him a long kiss. Jeremy closes his eyes tightly and savors every moment of the embrace.

Meanwhile, outside Brett and Jeff are speaking to each other so loud that everyone around them can easily hear them. Brett's voice continues to grow in both intensity and volume as he speaks, "Dude, you're not going to do it, so stop saying you will. It's really starting to irritate me. You've been saying you're going to jump off that thing all night, either do it or shut up about it." Brett emphatically puts his hands up in the air to let Jeff know that he is completely finished with this discussion. Jeff looks at him and grins, "Well, then I think it's time to put up or shut up!"

"So you're going to do it?"

"Yup, right now. No more talking; it's time for some action." Jeff stands up from the table and takes off his shirt. He whips it around his head and shouts out loudly, "Alright, if anyone wants to see the show, please make your way outside to the backyard. The program will begin shortly!"

He launches his shirt into the crowd of people around him and storms out the back door. He emerges from the house and is instantly hit by the warm night air. He breathes in deeply, steeling himself for what he is about to do.

Jeff has always been a bit of a wild man; in fact, that's what everyone loves about him. There isn't anything Jeff won't do. One of the most memorable times was when Jeff brought a shopping cart to school. Everyone thought that it was a bit odd, but he just told as many kids as he could to come out to the parking lot at the end of the day to see something cool. Naturally, what he was going to do was not going to very smart and could likely lead to physical damage, but he didn't care. So of course, everyone wanted to see what he was going to do. As a crowd gathered, Jeff marched his way over to the parking lot with the shopping cart. He aimed the cart towards the end of the parking lot, which abutted the baseball field. There was a lip at the end of the parking lot where it met the fence just before the field. No one could really figure out what he was doing. Then suddenly, he took off. He pumped his legs as hard as he could to reach his top speed and then hopped into the cart. The cart struck the lip and launched high into the air clearing the top of the fence by only a few inches. Jeff threw his hands up into the air triumphantly as he and the cart crashed hard into the outfield. The force of the impact ejected him a few feet from the cart. He promptly leaped to his feet and started jumping up and down like he had just won a million dollars. Everyone watching cheered and applauded the incredible accomplishment.

Here he is, at it again. Brett streaks around the inside of the house telling everybody that Jeff is about to do something insane in the backyard. Partygoers stream outside, anticipating something fantastic from the wild man, Jeff.

Jeff, ever the showman, takes his time stretching from one side to the other then begins to act like he is warming up for some sort of sporting event. He addresses the crowd before him, "Brett has informed me that no one has done this before and that he thinks it cannot be done. To that I say, Ha! I will now complete said challenge!"

The crowd's full attention is on Jeff as he turns and strides confidently towards the pool. He continues past the pool and starts to walk to a shed that is about ten feet away. He arrives at the shed and begins to climb. Jeff grabs a hold of the roof with his right hand and hoists the rest of his body up. As he stands on the top of the roof, looking out at the mass of people, Jeff can feel that all eyes are on him. He elevates his arms, "I will now leap from this rooftop to the pool!" People in the crowd raise their cups and start hollering, "You can do it, Jeff!"

83

"You got this!"

"You're the man, Jeff!"

Jeff takes a few steps back and lines himself up. In actuality, he isn't positive that he can make the jump, but he feels pretty confident that he has a good chance. Despite that, he is not afraid. He is completely absorbed in the attention of the moment.

He stands there on the top of the shed drinking it all in for as long as he can. His adrenaline is at full strength, blood speedily courses throughout his entire body as he readies himself for the jump. An instant later he takes off. He speeds towards the lip of the shed, knowing that he has to hit it at just the right point to get enough air to make it to the pool. He reaches the edge of the roofline and springs high into the air off his right foot. He stretches his legs out in front of him, willing his body to make it just a few more feet into the awaiting water.

Splash! He clears the lip of the pool by no more than a few centimeters. The crowd erupts. Jeff emerges from the water with his hands held victoriously over his head to the sound of cheers and clapping. Suddenly, a number of people in the crowd surge forward and bound into the pool, joining him in his celebration.

Lauren pulls her lips away from Jeremy's for a moment. "What is that?"

Jeremy, who is completely engrossed in the thralls of the kiss, hadn't heard any of the commotion going on right outside the window. "I don't know what you're talking about. What is what?"

"You don't hear that? It's coming from the backyard." Lauren stands up from the bed and walks over to the window. "Jeremy, come here. Check this out!"

Jeremy begrudgingly gets up from his spot on the bed and shuffles his way over to the window. He moves the blinds back out of the way with his hand and looks out.

The scene before them is pure jubilation. Throngs of kids are in the pool, frolicking and splashing each other. Zach and Brett have Jeff hoisted up on their shoulders in the shallow end of the pool. Jeff has a look of pure victory on his face and is pointing and laughing with those surrounding him. Jeremy looked to Lauren, "I wonder what Jeff did this time."

"That guy is crazy, Jeremy. I can't believe that he never gets hurt."

The truth is, no one understands how Jeff can do all of these insane things and never get injured. He is just that type of guy. If anyone else tried the things he does, they would get seriously injured for sure, but not Jeff. That guy just seems to be impervious to injury.

"Let's head down there and check it out, but before we go, let me take one last look at you." Lauren looks over Jeremy's face, making sure that nothing stands out. She sways her head from side to side and takes it all in. "I think you're ok. It's pretty dark out there anyway."

Jeremy thanks her. "How about one more kiss before we head out?"

Lauren smiles and the two kiss one last time before they leave the room and walk downstairs.

Brett sees Jeremy and Lauren emerge from the house, and sprints up to them. "Where were you guys? You missed it! Jeff jumped off the roof of the shed and into the pool! It was amazing! Then, everyone was so jacked up from the whole thing; people just started jumping into the pool. This is the best party ever!" With that, Brett peels away from them and jumps head first into the pool nearly crashing into a group of girls.

Jeff looks over his shoulder and sees Jeremy and Lauren talking to Brett. He proudly makes his way out of the pool and over to them. "Hey, did you see my jump?"

Jeremy shakes his head, "No, I'm so mad that I missed it. I heard it was pretty incredible."

Jeff wriggles his head, violently sending droplets of water flying in all directions. "It's cool. You know me. I didn't say I was done for the night."

Lauren's eyes bulge out of her head a bit, "You're going to do something else?"

Jeff looks at her and notices her eyes seem a little red, as if she's been crying, "Hey, are you ok? Your eyes look a little puffy, like you've been crying or something."

Jeremy quickly tries to change the subject, "Long story, but it's all good now. So what are you going to try next?"

86

Jeff forgets about his former curiosity. "For a long time now, I've wanted to try to make it to the pool by jumping off that roof. Tonight, I did. Mission accomplished. Well, there's something else I've always wanted to try, but I know Brett's parents will never let me attempt it. Guess what, my friend, there's no one here to stop me tonight!" Jeff puts his hands on Jeremy's shoulders and turns him in the direction of the other side of the yard. It is pretty dark out and there are no lights on that side of the yard. Jeremy struggles to see what Jeff is trying to point him towards.

"I don't see anything." Jeremy then realizes that he doesn't need to be able to see. He has been in this yard a thousand times before. It just takes him a minute to remember what is on that side of the yard. Then, it hits him. He quickly turns to face Jeff, "No way; that could be really dangerous."

"Danger is my middle name, my friend."

"No, it's not. It's Franklin. Right now, you have a very stupid idea forming in your head that may lead to your death."

It sounds a bit odd to have a name like Jefferson Franklin Sanders, but his dad is a complete history nut and decided to name him Jefferson Franklin after two of his favorite former presidents: Thomas Jefferson and Franklin D. Roosevelt. Believe it or not, Jeff's mom was actually ok with it.

Jeff continues, "Listen, I've got this. Why don't you do me a favor and just sit back, relax and enjoy the show with Lauren." Jeff walks over to the pool and jumps in. He swims over to a few of the guys who promptly get out of the pool. After a few minutes, there is a small group of boys standing on the outside of the pool waiting for Jeff. He exits the pool and turns to face those that remain in the pool.

"Tonight, I have done what has never been done before."

The people in the pool cheer.

"That was just a warm-up for the main attraction, which is going to take place in just a few moments. In order for this incredible feat to happen, I need a little help from the audience. I need everyone to please exit the pool at this time."

Whispers and conversation ripple throughout the anxious crowd as they exit the pool and wait.

Jeff and the other guys walk towards the other side of the yard and disappear into the darkness.

Jeremy looks at Lauren, "He's had a lot of really bad ideas, but this one may take the cake."

Moments later, the boys reemerge from the darkness dragging a very large circular object with them. Instantly everyone roars in excitement. The guys set down the trampoline a few feet from the shallow end of the pool.

Jeff's plan seems simple; get up as high as possible and then dive into the deep end of the pool. He knows that the higher he goes, the deeper he is going to plunge, which is why he is targeting the deepest part of the pool as his landing site. Jeff jumps on top of the

88

trampoline and addresses the crowd, "I am sure this is dangerous, but I laugh in the face of danger. I am sure that some of you right now may be thinking that I am crazy. Well, maybe I am a little nutty, but it sure is fun isn't it!"

The mass of people cheer loudly. He slowly starts to bounce on the trampoline, getting higher and higher each time his feet propel upwards off of the mesh material. He gets up to a good height and starts to speak again, "If I don't make it, tell my mom I love her!"

Jeff jumps a few more times getting as much height out of each bounce as he can. He takes one last massive jump and thrusts himself forward. He is at an absolutely staggering height as his body soars towards the water.

Everyone watches with baited breath as he flies through the air, passing the shallow end and surging on towards the deeper end of the pool. It seems like he is in the air for an eternity. The whole scene reminds Jeremy of those parts of movies where they slow everything down to a snail's pace so the audience can really take in the full weight of the moment.

Jeff lands hard into the water, creating a massive splash and sending waves of water out from his landing spot in all directions. He shoots down almost immediately to the bottom of the pool. He quickly angles his body so that, rather than crashing, he is able to skim the floor of the pool. The rough surface of the pool's bottom scrapes against his chest as he body continues to propel forward. He resurfaces over ten feet away from where he made impact. After the shed jump, the crowd cheered loudly. This time, the crowd went absolutely nuts.

Everyone swarmed into the pool and surrounded Jeff. Guys high-fived him repeatedly and girls rushed up to talk to him. He has achieved his goal: he has become the central focus of the entire party. Someone, somewhere, cranks the music up outside and the party resumes in full stride.

An hour or so later, Jeremy, Zach, Brett, Ricky, and Walter make a fire in the outdoor fire pit. They sit around the blaze, watching the flames and talking about what a great night it is, except for what happened to Jeremy, of course. As the party comes to a close, Brett kicks up his feet and rests them on the edge of the fire pit. "What a night! I mean, Jeremy gets punched in the noggin, but then ends up with the girl."

Lauren blushes and squeezes in a little closer to Jeremy.

Brett continues, "Jeff jumps off the roof and then the trampoline into the pool, both things I'd never try." Jeff stands up and takes a quick bow as Brett pretends like he's worshiping him. "And we have a kicking party where no cops show up, no one gets in any trouble, and no one breaks anything. Pretty incredible night, if I do say so myself."

Walter is sitting next to Zach looking completely distraught. "I can't believe it. I just can't believe it. A guy is a few hours late to a party, and he misses all the good stuff. This sucks."

90

Zach tosses a stick into the roaring fire, "It's no big deal, Walter. Jeff will do those things again, so you can see them too."

"That's not as good. Everyone's already seen it the first time it happened. I missed it because I wanted to beat some stupid game, which I did beat, if any of you were wondering. Damn it! I wish I had been here for all that!"

Ricky chuckles, "To be honest, you did miss all the good stuff."

"Thanks for that, Ricky. Like I'm not already pissed about it."

"Hey, now you know; never be late to a party. You never know what's going to happen."

They sit outside for a little while longer and enjoyed the warmth of the fire and the great company. Jeremy looks from face-to-face, each one lit up by the licking flames of the fire. He wonders; if he did go to St. Michael's, would he miss stuff like this? Would he be going to different parties with new friends? He really loves these guys; he has known them just about his entire life. Zach had proven to be more than just a regular type of friend tonight. He has shown that he is a guy that Jeremy can really trust if he is in a bind. The guy charged into a fight, not caring about anything other than the fact that his friend was in trouble and needed him. Jeremy looks at Zach, who is still busting on Walter for being late. The decision where to go to school next year, which is a big decision regarding Jeremy's future, appears to be so easy for his parents to make, has just become even more complicated.

The fire shrinks from a bright orange roaring flame to something that is barely emitting any light or heat. Jeremy stands up and stretches, "Well, fellas, I think I'm going to call it a night. We've got our first captain's practice in like five hours. So, I think we should all try and get at least some sleep."

The rest of the guys agree and stand up. Brett walks over to the water hose, turns it on, and douses the fire. He makes sure it is completely out before he joins the others in the house. Brett looks at the guys, "Well, now it's time for you all to figure out who's going to sleep where. Two of you can crash in my room; one can go on the floor the other on the loveseat.

Walter and Zach look to each other and sprint full speed up the stairs. Brett follows them with his eyes, "Ok, my room is now full. There's nothing else upstairs, so it's either find a spot in the living room on a couch, or look for a soft spot on the floor somewhere. I'll set my alarm for seven and wake all you guys up. See you in a few hours." With that, he trudges up the stairs and into his room.

Lauren faces Jeremy, "I'm going to go into Nicole's room and get some sleep. Call me or text me when you get out of practice, ok? She leans in, gives him a kiss, and then walks upstairs.

Jeff is next to leave, "I saw a comfy spot on the couch in the living room. I'm claiming that for me. See you guys in the A.M."

Ricky takes a look at Jeremy's face, "Hey, you may want to toss some more ice on that before you go to sleep. It's looks like it's

92

swelling up a bit." Jeremy accepts his friend's advice and walks into the kitchen. He opens the freezer door and takes out the same bag of peas he used before. He closes the door and takes a seat at the table. Ricky sits down next to him. Jeremy can tell he wants to say something because Ricky is sitting there awkwardly looking around the room, picking at his finger nails. Jeremy puts the peas on his nose and eyes. "What's up? It looks like you want to say something."

Ricky takes in a deep breath and lets it out loudly. "Look, I'm just sorry that I wasn't there to help take care of that punk tonight. You know I've always got your back. You and your parents mean everything to me."

"I know that. It's all good. I'm just glad that Zach got there when he did. I think he's way stronger than he was during the season. He's going to crush people next year."

Ricky laughs, "Yeah, that guy is turning into a total beast."

The two sit there a little while longer. "Ok, I think this is as about as good as it's going to get for tonight." Jeremy takes the bag and tosses it back into the freezer. "I think there's still some room on the floor in the living room. Want to head in?"

Ricky heaves himself out of the chair and follows Jeremy into the living room. Jeremy searches and finally finds a good spot on the ground next to a recliner. Ricky stumbles around a few sleeping bodies before he finally settles on a spot of his own. The two fall asleep as soon as their heads hit the floor.

8

The alarm sounds loudly in Brett's room. His hand fumbles around on the nightstand before finally connecting with its target. He groans and slams the snooze button on the alarm. Walter's head sticks up off the floor, "What's that?"

Brett looks down at his friend, "It's the alarm you fool. You've got ten more minutes of sleepytime before we've got to get moving."

Zach, unfazed by the alarm, rolls over and continues snoring lightly. Ten minutes later, the alarm booms to life again. This time, Brett smashes the off button and sits up. He shifts his legs so that they are hanging off of his bed and looks to the floor. Walter has also woken up with the second sounding of the alarm and is busily wiping the corners of his eyes. Zach is in the same position as before, still sleeping soundly. Brett turns to his right and grabs a pillow. He rifles the pillow at Zach and connects with his head. The pillow bounces off his head and crashes into the wall behind him. Zach opens one eye and glares at Brett, "If you do that again, I'm going to have to break you in half."

"It's time to get up. Come on let's go wake up the rest of the crew." Brett gets up and walks over to his dresser. He rips out a T-shirt and tosses it on. He pulls open another drawer and takes out a pair of shorts. He puts those on over his boxers, takes out a pair of socks, and heads out the door. He checks in the living room and sees bodies strewn about all over the floor. He kicks Ricky gently in the arm and wakes him up. He punches Jeff in the shoulder, who just laughs, and then walks over to Jeremy. "Let's go, QB. It's time to get moving."

Jeremy rolls over and faces Brett who winces. "Yikes! That doesn't look great."

"Does it look that bad?"

"Well, let's just say that it doesn't look good."

"Great, that's just what I need." Jeremy gets up and goes to look for his bag. The rest of the guys get ready and meet out on the front lawn.

"Nice shiner, Savvy!" shouts Zach. "It makes you look tough, just like me. Well, except without all of the muscles."

"Thanks, buddy," said Jeremy, "I'm going to run home and change real quick. I'll meet you guys at the field, ok?"

"You can't go home like that. What are you going to say to your mother?" asks Ricky.

Ricky was right. Jeremy thinks for a moment, "Brett, can I borrow some clothes?"

"Sure, just go upstairs to my room and grab whatever you want."

"Do you have an extra pair of cleats too?"

"Jeez, why don't you just take my entire closet while you're at it? Yeah, there should be another pair of cleats in my closet somewhere."

"Thanks! While I'm in the house changing, I'll call my mom and let her know that I won't be home until after practice. That should buy me some time to come up with a story." Jeremy takes off inside the house. He reemerges from the front door only a few minutes later and together, the guys begin the trek into the awaiting sunshine.

Time flies by swiftly as they walk to the field while talking about all of the craziness from the night before. They arrive at the field and see a few guys stretching out. Some others players are tossing a ball around near the sideline. This practice isn't an actual practice for the team just yet; those don't start for two more weeks. This is what is typically referred to as a captain's practice. Since the coaches can't start to have formal practices until a set date, the captains call a practice to get the guys together before the official start. It's not exactly mandatory, but it's definitely frowned upon if you don't show up. This goes double if you're a freshman.

The guys join the larger group and look around. Three kids stride up to them, obviously the captains. One guy, the biggest, steps out from the others, "Hey, I'm Clifton Williams. This is Sean Tate and Daniel Jacobs. We are going to be your captains this season. Clifton is a massive individual, standing taller than Jeremy and much thicker. Sean and Daniel are nowhere near as physically imposing as Clifton, but their faces show that they mean business.

Clifton continues, "I know this is your first practice, but we take this crap seriously. Don't come out here and think we are going to be messing around for a few hours because we aren't. I don't know about you guys, but I'm sick and tired of the reputation Centerville has and I fully intend to change it, so that's exactly what I'm going to do-with or without your help." He stares directly at Jeremy, "I hear you are some sort of superstar. Well, guess what, superstar? You haven't been hit by me or anyone like me yet, but you will. I hope you're ready for the pain because this ain't junior league any more. Judging from that black eye on your face, it looks like someone already got started on you."

Zach can hardly contain himself. He is completely focused on every single word that is coming out of Clifton's mouth. Clifton looks imposingly at Zach, "What are you looking at, Freshman?"

"Nothing. I just can't wait to go out there and hit someone. I'm just feeling a little psyched up right now." Clifton takes a moment and looks Zach up and down, nodding in approval as he does so, "Looks like you've been hitting the gym a bit. That's good because on my defense, I don't want anyone that can't bring it. This year, this is my defense, and we ain't taking crap from anyone."

Clifton steps in really close to Zach, nearly standing face-to-face with him, "On my defense something runs near you, I want you to crush it. You see a quarterback other than our own, you annihilate him. A running back tries to get by you, you take him out. A wide receiver goes across the middle or tries to make a catch, you hit him so hard he forgets his name. You get me?"

"Oh yeah!" Zach responds emphatically.

Clifton looks over his shoulder to Sean, "I think I like this one." He turns back to face the group, "Other than QB over here and maybe Goodman, the rest of you probably won't see much game time other than in the freshman games. But that doesn't mean you slack on our practice field. You play every down hard, or you will have to answer to me. Now join the rest of the guys out on the field, so we can get this thing going."

The captains lead the team out onto the field and start the warm-up. Jeremy can feel the heat of the summer sun on his face as he cranes his neck up, completing a stretch. He can already tell that it is going to be a scorcher today with temperatures reported to creep into the nineties. Clifton raises his hand up high over his head, "Ok! Defense with me; offense follow Sean and Daniel. Some of you freshman might not be sure exactly where to go. I can help you with that. If you want to hit something come with me, if not, get as far away from me as possible and go over there with them."

The team splits up into two squads and practices on drills and technique. The sun beats down from a cloudless sky, and sweat begins to pour off of the athletes as they continue to work. Although it is their first practice, the majority of the freshmen are able to hold their own during the first part of the practice.

After a few hours, the captains call for a water break. Jeremy wearily walks over where the coolers are located and grabs a paper cup. He pulls the knob on the cooler marked 'water' and fills up the cup. He lifts the cool water to his lips and pours the liquid down his throat. He grabs another cup of water, but this time he spills the entire contents over his head in an attempt to cool himself off. A little chill courses through his body as the water drips off of his wet hair and falls haplessly to the dry ground.

Walter is sitting under a nearby tree, looking like he may pass out at any moment. Jeff and Jake are busily taking in as much water as they can while Brett stands tiredly talking to Larry next to the tables that are holding the coolers. Even the upperclassmen seem like they need a break. Out of the entire group, there are only two people on the field that seem unfazed by the heat and the amount of energy expelled to this point: Zach and Clifton.

Clifton continues to discourse with Zach regarding something that happened just before the break. It is obvious to Jeremy that Clifton is taking to Zach, most likely because of Zach's strength and eagerness to learn.

From what Jeremy was able to see from across the field, no one seems able to block Zach. On top of that, it seems like Zach is bulling over and through just about any and every target Clifton puts in front of him, no matter how big or tough the other guy is.

Once Clifton feels that Zach understands what he is trying to say, he changes his attention to the group, "Alright, guys. It's time to put up or shut up. Seven-on-seven drills. There is going be no tackling of any kind, coach will absolutely kill me if one of you ding-dongs gets

99

injured before we even start double sessions in a few weeks. If it looks like you don't know what you're doing out there, we will replace you with someone that does. On offense, there will be two linemen: the center and a guard. Opposing them will be two defenders; they can either be standing up or with their hand in the dirt. I have no problem with contact on the line of scrimmage; in fact, I encourage there to be a little bit of it. I want to see if any of you new guys have any toughness." Clifton pauses for a second to toss back a cup full of water. He crinkles up the cup and flings it in the direction of the coolers.

He continues, "On offense, outside of the center and guard we will be using a QB, one running back, and three wide receivers. If you play tight end, we will work you in based on offensive packages, but the majority of the drill will be featuring three wide outs. We need to showcase this new gem of a quarterback we have. On D, we've got the two linemen, two backers, and three backfield players. There could be any variation that I feel like calling from three corners, to one corner and two safeties. I need to see if you can play in some man-on-man situations. Remember gentlemen, there are only seven guys out there on a side. If you get smoked, it's going to be really obvious to everyone watching. Ok, let's get started."

In the first two hours of practice, Jeremy assesses his offensive weapons. One of the receivers, Lance, has pretty decent hands, but not nearly enough speed to run anything outside of twenty yards down the field. Ricky, however, has been having a great practice. He is running faster than anyone and catching everything. Sean and Daniel both play a little bit of running back and wide receiver. To be honest, Jeremy really isn't impressed with either of them, but they are running the practice well and know all of the plays by heart.

The offense forms a huddle, and Sean calls a play. Jeremy nods, quickly analyzing all of the routes of the play, and strides to the line of scrimmage. The center grabs the ball and waits for the call from Jeremy. The ball is snapped to Jeremy. He takes his familiar three-step drop. The play is going to take about four seconds to fully develop and relies on perfect timing between Sean and Daniel on a crossing route.

Reacting to the snap of the ball, Clifton back-peddles and tries to diagnose what is unfolding before him. He can see Daniel and Sean angling towards one another and yells out that it is a crossing route. Before Jeremy is able to get the ball out of his hand, he is slapped hard on the shoulder by something flying by him.

Zach beats the man in front of him easily and touches Jeremy to indicate a sack. While returning back to the line, Zach gloats past Jeremy, "That makes one, QB. Better get that ball out faster next time." Zach saunters back to the defensive side and gets a round of high fives from Clifton and the rest of the defensive unit.

Daniel gets down on one knee in the center of the huddle, "How about we block the kid long enough to actually run the play this time? Jeremy, we're going to go overload left. Look for the post route." They hustle up to the line. The ball is snapped to Jeremy. He takes it and makes a quick drop back. He pump fakes once and let's go of a perfect spiral towards the streaking receiver. Sean gets just enough separation to have a half-step lead on the defensive back. The ball sails over the defender and into Sean's hands for a long gain.

Sean, now feeling a bit cocky, says, "Hey, Clifton, I think we should make this a little more interesting. How about this? Let's cut the field in half to fifty yards. Offense gets four downs to make it to the end zone. Every time we score, we get six points. Every time you hold us from scoring, you get three points. You guys also get one point for every sack, and two for every interception. What do you think?"

Clifton, never one to turn down a challenge, gladly accepts the proposition and starts preparing his defense for the competition. Clifton turns his head to face Sean, "Hey, what are we playing up to?"

Sean looks to Daniel and thinks for a moment, "Why don't we play for a set amount of time, and whoever has the lead at the end wins?"

"Ok, ten-minute quarters, running clock."

Sean nods his head in agreement and readies the offense. Daniel looks at Sean, "Four downs to go fifty yards? Are you nuts?"

"Stop whining! We've got the Golden Boy here at QB don't we?" Sean stares hard at Jeremy, "Look, kid. This is how you earn your stripes. I don't want to lose to Clifton. We will never hear the end of it, trust me. So, let's take it to him, ok?"

Jeremy nods and gets himself ready.

Clifton barks out a play and leads his team to the line of scrimmage.

As the offense comes to set, Jeremy locks his eyes on the ball, which is grasped in the center's hand. "Set, go!" The ball is tossed back to Jeremy. He takes a few steps back and scans the field. The linemen collide as the defenders try to reach Jeremy, while his offense strains to protect him. Jeremy shuffles one step to his right and launches a pass deep down the field to a wide open receiver. Ricky catches the ball and is tagged a few yards later for about a twenty-yard gain.

In the offensive huddle, Sean struggles to contain his excitement, "Wow Savvy! You've got a rocket-launcher for an arm. Daniel, let's call something long and see if we can get in the endzone right here."

Daniel flips through the plays in his mind for a moment and calls a play.

The offense gets to the line and sets up for the next play. Jeremy taps his foot, sending one of the receivers into motion. Once the receiver is set, the ball is snapped. Jeremy drops back and scans the field from left to right. Zach makes an incredible spin move to get around the guard and streaks for Jeremy. Out of the corner of his eye, Jeremy sees Zach and rocks back on his feet. He makes a quick juke move and slides to his left. Once he is by Zach, he sets his feet and hones in on his target.

Lance gets past his defender and is striding towards the end zone. The ball flies effortlessly out of Jeremy's hand, carving its way through the air towards Lance. Lance doesn't have to make any adjustments as Jeremy's pass lands perfectly in his hands, hitting him right in stride. Lance spikes the ball in the endzone and celebrates as his teammates rush to him.

Clifton spins around wildly, searching for the one responsible. He runs over to the cornerback and grabs him by the shirt. "You call that defense?" Clifton shoves him hard towards the sideline. "I need someone else. You! Let's go."

Jeff hasn't really been paying attention to what was taking place on the field. He is still busily talking to Brett about his incredible jump into the pool from the roof of the shed when Clifton points at him.

"Hey, you! I'm talking to you. You want to play or not?"

Jeff does a double-take and points to himself. "Are you talking to me?"

"Yeah, you. You in or not?"

"Heck, yeah! I'm in." Jeff sprints towards the field and gets into the defensive huddle.

On the offensive side, the enthusiasm is palpable. Sean looks at Daniel, "This kid might be the best I've ever seen. Did you see those two throws? On the money."

Daniel smirks, "I know. Let's see if he can make this one."

104

Daniel calls out the next play, and the offense rushes up to the line of scrimmage. "What's the matter Clifton? Not ready yet?"

Clifton glowers over his shoulder, "Shut up, Danny, before I come over there and stomp on your head." He turns back to face his defense. "That was pathetic, we need to do better! I'm not going to get embarrassed by these guys."

The defense lines up and gets ready. The ball is snapped back, and once again, Jeremy takes his perfected three-step drop, as the play unfolds before him. Zach, rather than going around the guard this time, decides to bull-rush right through him, knocking the guard off of his feet as he continues on towards Jeremy.

Zach raises an outstretched hand in the air, trying in vain to knock down the ball that is making its way out of Jeremy's hand. The ball nicks Zach's fingertip, but it is not enough to throw it off target. The throw scorches through the air at an amazing speed and lands in Sean's hands as he crosses the endzone line easily.

Back in the huddle, Clifton pats Zach on the back, "I saw that. Nice try. You were almost there. Damn, that kid can really chuck it."

Zach replies, "Haven't you seen any of his games? Jeremy is a prodigy, like the once-in-a-generation type."

"What is he doing out here with us? He should be playing at St. Michael's."

Zach laughs, "Yeah right! Jeremy, at that preppy school? I don't think so. Besides, we're all best friends. He wouldn't just leave us like that."

"You sure about that? I've played with guys that have done exactly that a number of times."

Zach scoffs, "Savvy's not like that, and he would have told us by now if he was going there. Plus, he's here practicing, isn't he?"

"Well, based off of what I've just seen, I hope you're right. We can really go far with a guy like that. Anyway, we are getting killed out there, so it's time to change some things up. The only linebacker on the field is going to be me. We are going to go with two corners and a pair of safeties over the top; no more deep stuff allowed. They've only got four guys going out on routes, and we have five to defend them. Let's do this!"

With the score 12-0, the offense struts confidently up to the line of scrimmage. The ball is snapped, and the defense drops back into their new coverage. Jeremy, doesn't see anyone open, so he tries to buy time for the wide outs to break free. He steps to his right, then left, but nothing opens up. He finally gets tagged by Zach. "Yeah! one for us!"

Jeremy looks at him, "Nice play, Zach. Way to stay with it."

"Thanks, Savvy. You're a pain in the neck to track down, though!"

As the game continues, the new defense proves to be more effective as they consistently have more defenders out on the field than

106

the offense has receivers. The score is 24-22 as the two sides prepare for the final drive of the day. If the defense can hold them, they will win the game; but if the offense scores, then they will be victorious. Clifton shouts out to his defense as the offense lines up. The ball is snapped back to Jeremy. He takes three steps back and quickly unloads a perfect spiral to Daniel running a slant route. Daniel catches the ball and is tagged almost immediately. The play goes for a ten-yard gain; three downs left to go forty yards.

In the huddle, Sean and Daniel converse regarding the next play. "I think we should keep moving the ball up field. I don't think we need go for the home run yet," said Sean.

Daniel ponders this and calls the next play. As the ball is being snapped to Jeremy, Ricky loses his footing and falls hard to the ground. Jeremy sees this and changes his read on the play. He slide-steps to his right, avoiding the attacking Zach, and zips a pass out to Sean on a corner route. Sean catches the ball for a twenty-yard gain and is tagged by the safety to stop the play.

"One minute left!" someone shouts out from the sideline. Clifton yells out to his defense, "Third down! They've got to go another twenty yards. Nothing behind you!" The ball is hiked back to Jeremy who spins it in his hands and lines up his fingers with the laces. The deep routes are well-covered, leaving him only two other options. He pumps once, then twice, and finally let's go of a short pass, which is caught by Ricky for about seven yards.

"Thirty seconds!" The guys on the sideline are hooting and hollering, cheering for their respective side. The offense speedily huddles and jogs to the line. Jeremy checks the coverage the defense is in and calls for the ball. He takes it and goes through his progressions. Sean and Daniel are well-covered. This leaves Ricky and Lance as his only targets. Jeremy looks off Ricky and plants his back foot, preparing to unload a pass to Lance.

Zach makes an incredible swim move to get around the guard. He takes three long strides and leaves his feet, plunging through the air towards Jeremy with his hands outstretched. As Jeremy releases the ball from his hand, Zach's fingers come into contact with the ball and send it wobbling off target. The ball spins at odd angles and eventually lands on the ground, bouncing this way and that, sealing a victory for the defense. Zach lands hard on the ground. His body, unable to defend itself, makes vicious contact with the unrelenting turf, but it doesn't matter. He leaps back up to his feet and celebrates. Clifton rushes over to him and heaves him up, "Nice play Zach!" Clifton looks over at Daniel, "Good game, but the D wins this time!"

Once the celebration is over, the captains call the team together. Clifton addresses them, "Not bad today fellas. Not bad at all. Some of you, like Zach over here, have really impressed me. Some of you have a lot of work to do if you want to see any real time on the field. I'll see you all again tomorrow morning, same time."

108

Daniel stands up and gestures for the team to huddle around him, "Hands in guys, hands in. Centerville on three: one, two, three, Centerville!"

With that, Jeremy's first ever captain's practice comes to an end.

9

Three days into the captains' practices, Walter is already talking about quitting. "I suck. I can't keep up with anyone, and for the majority of practice, I feel like I'm going to have a heart attack! The captains are always yelling at me. I feel like I can't do anything right out there." Walter flings an arm into the water in frustration, sending droplets of water shooting out in all directions.

Zach inches his body up on his float, he is enjoying the much needed rest after another grueling day of practice. "Relax, Walter. You're getting much better out there. Plus, you just started hitting the gym. It's going to take a little while to build up your strength and stamina. Watch. A few weeks from now, you're going to feel completely different, I promise. By the time I am done with you, you're going to be running circles around most of those guys out there. The ones you can't run circles around, you're going to be crushing."

Jeremy's head emerges from the water; he shakes the water out of his ears and finds a float of his own to rest on. He tosses his tired body onto the float and lets out an audible sigh as he feels his body begin to relax.

The last few days had done wonders for the injury to Jeremy's eye. The swelling is completely gone, and the color is fading fast. The tricky part of the equation was convincing his mother that it had happened at practice. To Jeremy's amazement, Zach had come up with an entire story where he accidentally hit Jeremy in the face as he was about to throw the ball. He even apologized again to Jeremy in front of her while telling the story. Jeremy had to admit, the story was so good that he would have believed it too.

Zach looks over at Jeremy, "Can you please tell Walter that he is looking good out there and to have a little patience."

The heat is burning up Jeremy's skin. He takes one of his legs off the float and plunges it into the cool water, taking his body temperature down a bit. "Walter, you may not be noticing the way you're playing, but we are. You are much better than you were last year, and you had your best practice ever today. You made some great plays out there," says Jeremy.

"You guys are great friends, but you're also both full of crap. I'll be lucky to see time on the freshman squad nevermind JV." Walter rolls off of his float and sinks to the bottom of his pool. He exhales a little out of his nose and watches as the bubbles meander through the water forcing their way to the surface. He looks up to see the water over his head, which the bright sun has turned to a beautiful shade of turquoise. He always finds the calmness of the water to be so relaxing. He stays there, weightless, for a few more seconds and then moves his arms and legs, forcing his body to the surface.

Walter's head materializes from out of the water. The sun warms his face. Walter leans his head back and absorbs all of the suns' rays that he can. He kicks his legs gently, keeping his body afloat. The

111

practices have been really taking a toll on him lately. After today's long and arduous practice, the pool feels incredible to Walter, completely rejuvenating his once exhausted body. "I don't know; maybe I should just quit."

Zach is completely incensed by the mere notion of Walter quitting. He can't stand quitters. There is no way he is going to let his best friend give up on something that he knows Walter wants to be a part of just because it's tough.

Zach spins his head around to face Walter so fast it almost sends him off his float. "You're not quitting! I won't let you do that. It's hard now, and it's going to get harder once we start two-a-days, but you're not quitting, so get that stupid thought right out of your head. Does it suck that you have to work harder than some of the other guys? Yeah, it does. But that doesn't mean that you just quit. Look at me. I used to be that little runt getting kicked around, and now look. I'm the one dealing out the punishment. I don't care how much time it takes, you and I are going to work hard in the gym to get you where you need to be. Trust me; you'll be shocked by what you'll be able to do soon."

The look on Zach's face drives home the point to Walter. Walter knows that Zach means every word he is saying. The guy is fiercely loyal to his friends and really would spend as much time with Water as he needed in order to be successful on the field.

Deep down Walter really doesn't want to quit. He has been struggling to keep up physically with everyone at practice, but he loves being around the guys. He also loves the game of football. The feeling of belonging to a team is something that he truly treasures. Perhaps it is because his father is never around, and the team has really become like his family. Floating there, he doesn't really know why he is even suggesting that he may quit. Maybe it is because he is just looking for some reassurance from a friend, or maybe he is hoping that either Zach or Jeremy has seen something at practice that will give him a sliver of hope for playing time this upcoming season.

This past season, Walter hardly ever got onto the field during a game. He is not looking forward to the prospect of another season of watching from the sidelines. To him, it has been painfully obvious that he isn't as fast or as strong as the other guys at practice. This did not come as a shock to Walter. What he has in intellectual ability, he lacks in athleticism. He knows that he does not have the physical gifts some of the other kids possess and that, in order to play, he is going to have to work much harder.

"I'm telling you, Walter, this was your best practice" said Jeremy. "You are a much better blocker than you think you are. If you keep working on your strength and footwork, you are going to be able to get some playing time. Plus, you're smarter than a lot of the other guys on the team. You've picked up the offense much faster than most of them. You comprehend it. Now, it's just a matter of getting your physical abilities to match your brain." Once Jeremy finishes, he leans back on his float and continues his relaxation.

113

Walter takes a moment to think about what Jeremy is saying to him. He begins to feel a little better. It is true; he does understand the offense. That much he is sure of. He does know where he is supposed to be on any given play at any given time. He hasn't made a single mistake on that in practice yet, where a lot of the other guys have. He feels like his blocking technique is getting a little better too.

"You guys really think today was my best practice?" A little glimmer of hope is evident Walter's tone.

"I'm telling you," says Jeremy, "you were really good out there today. You've just got to keep moving your feet when you block and keep that defender in front of you. Don't let him by you, no matter what."

"I had to work pretty hard today to get past you, Walter, so I know you had a good practice," says Zach.

"Thanks, guys, I really needed that."

"Anytime, buddy." Jeremy slides off of his float and trudges through the water towards the stairs. "I think it's about time I head home and get something to eat. I'm starving."

"We can order some food if you want. My dad, like always, left money on the table for me to eat dinner," says Walter.

"Thanks Walter, but I told my parents I'd be home for dinner."

Jeremy gets out of the water, grabs a towel, and dries off. "See you guys tomorrow at practice."

114

Zach looks over at Jeremy. "So, are you really going home, or are you blowing us off to go hang out with your girlfriend?" Zach laughs and sends a little splash in Jeremy's direction.

Jeremy smirks. He walks over to one of the lounge chairs and drapes the now wet towel on it to dry. "No, I'm really going home to eat. I am hoping to see her later, though."

"Aww, that's so cute!" says Zach.

"Shut up. You wish you had a girlfriend."

Walter laughs, "He's got you there, Zach."

"Yeah, yeah, yeah. I'm just busting you up Savvy, you know that."

"I know you are. It's all good. See you guys tomorrow morning."

Walter and Zach wave good-bye to Jeremy who has left the two of them floating lazily in the pool as he walks away. He looks around the beautiful yard as he paces towards the house. He really hopes that Walter takes what he said seriously. Walter is a great guy, and Jeremy would hate to see him quit the team, whether he plays at Centerville or not. Jeremy continues walking, exits through the front door, and begins the walk home.

10

From down the street, Jeremy can see a strange car sitting in his driveway. He does a quick memory scan to see if he can recall who it belongs to, but comes up blank. He continues walking towards the house. He slowly walks up the steps leading to the front door and announces his arrival as he opens the door.

"Mom, I'm home."

"We are in the kitchen, honey. Why don't you come in? There's someone here that would like to see you." Sitting at the kitchen table are both of Jeremy's parents and Coach Fletcher. A look of surprise passes over Jeremy's face. "Hey, Coach."

"Hello Jeremy, it's nice to see you again." The coach stands up from his seat and extends a hand towards Jeremy, who shakes it firmly. Coach looks at Jeremy's dad and smiles, "Your son has one heck of a grip!"

David smirks and addresses his son. "We got a call from the coach this morning saying that he hadn't heard from you yet regarding your decision. So, he wanted to know if he could come by and discuss St. Michael's with us. You know, to see how we feel about everything."

Jeremy slowly nods his head up and down and takes a seat at the table. Coach speaks, "Look, Jeremy, I know it's only been a few days since we last talked, but my captains have already started getting the

116

team together for drills. I'd like you to be involved as early as possible; this way they can get you ready for the season. If it's ok with you, I'll give them your number and have one of them call you tonight to tell you where to go and what time to be there."

"Well, I've been practicing with Centerville so far. You know, with all the guys I know from the team and everything," says Jeremy.

"I understand that. Those are the guys that you know best; naturally, you want to be with them. But, it's definitely to your benefit if you are out there with the team as soon as you can be so that you can build some chemistry with the receivers and get to know the rest of your teammates. Your dad also said that you are going to the Direct Athletics Camp next week, which is incredible, by the way. I only know of a handful of athletes that have been invited there. All of them have turned out to be complete studs. But, by going there, you're going to miss a week of practice. I just don't want you to be too far behind when the real practices start."

As the coach sits there and waits for Jeremy to talk, he is taken aback by the fact that it truly seems like the kid hasn't made up his mind yet. Seriously, what is there to even consider? St. Michael's is better than Centerville High in every single way you can compare the two schools. When Jeremy first said that he had to think about it, the coach gave the impression that he understood. He did so fully anticipating that Jeremy would come to the "right" decision and call him later that night, the next day at the latest. But that didn't happen. Now, here he is, forced to take matters into his own hands.

Jeremy averts his eyes towards the floor and responds, "Well, I still haven't decided if I want to go to St. Michael's. I've been playing with the guys from Centerville to keep my game up and to meet some of the guys from the team. It's been fun so far."

David lets out an audible breath and crosses his arms. "Jer, the coach has been telling your mother and me about all of the incredible things they have at St. Michael's. Did you know they just finished construction on a new stadium? They even put down real field turf! Plus, they added a new weight room a few years back. Coach says it's nearly as big as some colleges'. They even have a film room exclusively for the football team to use in preparation for games. Pretty cool, huh?"

"Yeah, cool" says Jeremy.

The coach sits there, spinning around that championship ring in the same way he had done when he was talking to Jeremy and Ricky out on the field. He is completely dumfounded at this point. Why is this kid not shaking his hand right now? Why is Jeremy not telling him that he can't wait to play for him this fall?

The coach jumps back into the conversation, "Jeremy our facilities are unrivaled by any school in the area. At St. Michael's, we feel that it is our utmost priority to ensure that all of the athletes are provided with the tools they need to be successful. We even offer

118

specialized tutoring for athletes designed around their busy schedules. We take volunteers from our National Honor Society and link them up with any athlete that feels they need a little extra support in class. The results have been very encouraging."

"Jeremy's education is very important to us," says his mother. "His academics come first, then sports."

"Absolutely," said the coach. "St. Michael's is known for both its academic prowess and athletic dominance. We take great pride in that."

His mother smiles approvingly.

The coach thinks fast and comes up with one more tidbit to try and lure in Jeremy and his family. "You know, Jeremy, I've also spoken to our Dean. We don't usually do this, but he is willing to waive all charges for your tuition. You'll be able to attend the best high school in the area for absolutely nothing."

The three of them sit there quietly staring at Jeremy. They are seemingly waiting for him to say *something*.

An awkward silence fills the room. Jeremy continues to just sit there, wishing for this to be over. This whole conversation is making Jeremy feel uncomfortable. He feels like the three of them are just waiting for him to accept the offer to play at St. Michael's right now at the table. This way, they could move on to discussing the next steps. Something inside of him, however, is just not one hundred percent sure he wants to play there, despite the fact that they have the very best of everything.

Jeremy's mom senses his unease and speaks, "Well, Coach, I think that David and I have all the information we need from you. How about we let Jeremy have a break and relax a bit after that long practice. Jeremy, say bye to the coach, then run upstairs and take a shower while your father and I walk him out."

Jeremy silently thanks his mother for getting him out of this situation and jumps up from the table. He shakes the coach's hand again. "I look forward to hearing from you soon Jeremy" said the coach.

"Ok," says Jeremy. Then he turns and sprints up the stairs.

Jeremy's parents walk the coach to the door. "Mr. and Mrs. Savage, I just want to thank you for your time today. Your son's really going to be something special. I'd love it if I was the one that helped shape his football future. I truly feel, thanks to my own background and experiences, that I have the capability to help guide him on this journey."

David shakes the coach's hand. "Thanks for coming by today, Coach. I'm sure you'll be hearing from Jeremy really soon."

"I hope so."

The coach walks to his car and opens the driver's side door. He sits down and starts the engine, which roars to life immediately. He watches as the Savages wave, and eventually close the front door. He adjusts the rearview mirror and stares at his reflection.

I have to have this kid on my team.

Given the squad he has already, he feels confident that St. Michael's will be able to rip off consecutive state titles with Jeremy at the helm.

It is evident through today's conversation that the parents feel the same way he does. They seem to be enamored with the athletic facilities and academic reputation of St. Michael's. Tossing in the free tuition definitely shored up their support. However, for some reason, Jeremy is still having trouble with the decision. The coach has even offered for Jeremy's best friend, Ricky, to play at the school with him. This is something he isn't even quite sure will work out. Sure, Ricky has some speed and skills, but St. Michael's has a roster full of great athletes that can catch and run with the ball. But, if it means locking up a talent like Jeremy, it is something he is willing to do.

The coach continues to think as he backs out of the driveway. There has to be some other way to demonstrate to Jeremy that St. Michael's is not just the best, but the only choice for him. There has to be something that will show Jeremy that, no matter how good he may be, Centerville will never be on par with the best teams in the state. As he drives away from the house of the most talented quarterback he has ever laid eyes on, he continues to think. An idea forms in his head. The more he thinks of it, the more loves it. Yes, this will work. This *has* to work.

"Jeremy, can you come down here, please?" His father is standing at the bottom of the stairs. He has a look of utter befuddlement on his face. "Take it easy on him, David."

"It's not like I'm mad or anything, I just don't get it. Why is this such a tough decision for him?"

"He already told you, he doesn't want to leave his friends behind."

"That's cute and all, but now we are talking about his future. It's time that he grows up a bit and makes an adult decision."

"If you come at him like that, he's going to push back. Let's just talk to him, and see what he thinks."

Jeremy slowly walks from his room and down the stairs. He knows what is about to happen. He is not looking forward to this discussion at all. Every step Jeremy takes is excruciatingly slow, clearly demonstrating to his parents that he does not want to do this right now.

"What's up, Dad?"

"What was all that about? The coach was trying to talk to you, and you just sat there. Your mother and I were trying to converse with you, and you seemed like you couldn't be bothered."

"I don't know. It was weird."

"How was it weird, honey?" his mother asked softly.

"You guys were just all sitting there looking at me. It made me feel uncomfortable."

"Well, we were kind of waiting for you to accept the offer, so we could set you up with the captains for practice."

"I like practicing with Centerville. I know all those guys."

"True, but you'll know all the guys at St. Michael's as well, once you start practicing with them."

Jeremy exhales loudly and sits on the bottom step. "I just don't know where I want to go next year. I keep trying to tell you guys that I don't want to leave my friends behind. I understand that St. Michael's is a great school and has a lot to offer, but I'm still just not sure what I want to do."

Jeremy's dad rolls his eyes, "Jeremy, you're being a little silly about this whole thing. Those guys are still going to be your friends. You're just going to make new ones too. Would you only go to a college if all of your other friends were going?"

"No."

"Well, then?"

Jeremy's frustration begins to bleed into his words, "Dad, I don't know how else to tell you that I'm just not sure what I want to do yet. I know it's a great opportunity for me, but that doesn't make the decision any easier."

Jeremy's mother puts up her hand towards David, indicating for him to stop. "Jeremy, we love you, and we just want to make sure that

123

whatever you do, it's the best thing for you." She comes over to him and sits down next to him. She places an arm around his shoulder and leans her head on his. "I know this is a tough one for you. But, you know what? You take as much time as you need to make your decision. Don't feel like you're being pressured from the coach, us, or your friends."

"Thanks, Mom, but my friends don't even know that I'm even considering St. Michael's yet."

"I see. Well, maybe that's something you should talk to them about and see what they think." David shoots an icy look at his wife. "Do you really think that is smart, dear?" asks David.

"I do," she moves her eyes from David to Jeremy, "I also know that their opinions mean a lot to you. Talk to them; see what they think and how they feel. I'm willing to bet that if you ask them, each of them would still be your friend if you went to a different school."

"Maybe you're right, Mom. I'll talk to the guys tomorrow after practice."

"Good. Now, how about you go wash up, and your dad and I will start dinner?"

Jeremy gives her a kiss on the cheek and goes up the stairs.

His mother stands up from the step and walks passed David on her way to the kitchen. He asks, "Are you sure this is the best idea?"

"Listen, he's going to have to talk to them sooner or later, might as well make it sooner." As David is about to say something else, the phone rings. Jessica picks it up, "Hello?"

"Hello, is this Mrs. Savage?"

"Yes it is. May I ask who is calling?"

"This is Courtney Kearney from the mayor's office." Jessica's eyes open wide, and her mouth falls open. David, seeing this, mouths the words, "Who's that?" She covers the bottom of the phone, "It's the mayor's office."

"What do they want?"

"I don't know; you're talking to me so I can't hear her."

"I'm sorry, I didn't catch what you just said, could you please repeat that?" asks Jessica.

"Absolutely! I'm calling on behalf of Mayor Clinton Thompson. He wants me to schedule an appointment for you and your husband to meet with him at your earliest convenience."

"May I ask what this is in regard to?"

"He would like to talk with you about your son, Jeremy."

A look of confusion sweeps over Jessica's face, "I don't understand; is he in some sort of trouble?"

"No, not at all! He would just like to talk to you and your husband. How does tomorrow at 12 P.M. work for you?"

"Hold on one second." Jessica covers the mouthpiece on the phone again. "David, the mayor of Centerville wants to meet with you and me tomorrow."

"About what?"

"Jeremy."

"Why does the mayor want to talk to us about our son?"

"I don't know, but are we free tomorrow at noon?"

"I think so. Jeremy should still be at practice at that time, and I don't have summer school tomorrow."

Jessica removes her hand from the phone. "Tomorrow at twelve works for us."

"Excellent! I'll greet you at the receptionist desk tomorrow. See you then!"

Jessica hangs up the phone. She can't deny that she is a little excited and confused at the same time. The mayor wants to talk to her about her son. The *mayor*.

David is standing, confusedly shaking his head. "I don't get it. Why would he want to talk to us?"

"I don't know, but the two of us are meeting with the mayor tomorrow." Jessica smiles to herself, then thinks out loud, "What am I going to wear?"

Upstairs, Jeremy is on the phone talking to Lauren. "Hey, Lauren, there's something I've been wanting to talk to you about."

"What is it?"

"Um, I sort of, got an offer to go to St. Michael's next year to play football."

"Oh. Have you made a decision yet?"

"No. I can't make up my mind."

"Well, I'd be lying if I said it didn't matter to me where you went. Obviously, if you go to Centerville, I'll be able to see you a lot more, which is something that I'd really like."

Jeremy smiles to himself after hearing that. "I know. Me too. Plus, I've been hanging out with the same guys every day since I can remember. I really can't imagine not going to school with them anymore."

"It sounds like you have a lot to think about."

"Definitely. What do you think I should do?"

"That's not a decision for me to make. I mean, I've heard of St. Michael's. I know it's a really good school for sports and stuff, but I have no idea if you'd like it better than Centerville High or not."

"Yeah, I know, but I want to know what you think."

"I think that you should talk to your parents about it and see what they say."

"It's pretty clear; they think that I should go to St. Michael's."

"Oh. Well, I'm sure they have their reasons for feeling that way," Lauren says softly.

"But, I'm not sure that's what *I* want to do."

"I think that I'm a bad person for you to ask this question to, because I really like you, and I think that this relationship can turn into something pretty special. So, obviously, I'm going to want you to go to Centerville to be closer to me."

Jeremy is ecstatic that Lauren feels the same way he does. Since the party they have either talked or texted every night, sometimes for hours and hours at a time.

"I totally agree with you, I think that things are really going well between us" says Jeremy. "I really like having you as my girlfriend." The words came out faster than Jeremy had anticipated. The two of them hadn't actually discussed that topic just yet.

"Oh, so I'm your girlfriend now, huh? Don't even need to ask, I see."

Jeremy's cheeks flush. "I'm sorry. TLhat's not what I meant to say."

"So, you don't want me to be your girlfriend then? Wow, I guess you don't like me all that much." Lauren is enjoying teasing Jeremy. She knows that he is such a nice guy and is probably freaking out right now, but she wanted to let him stew a bit longer.

"No, of course I'd like you to be my girlfriend. I just guess I hadn't asked yet, but then I said that, and you kind of made it seem like maybe you didn't want to so…"

Lauren's laughter makes Jeremy stop dead in his tracks. "Relax Jeremy; I'm just messing with you. Yes, I'd love to be your girlfriend."

Relief washes over him. "That's great to hear. You really had me going, you know."

"Yeah, I know. You're way too easy to mess with. It's kind of fun, actually. Hey, what are you doing after practice tomorrow?"

"I don't know. Usually we just go to Walter's house and swim in the pool to cool off and relax after baking in the sun for hours and hours at practice. Why?"

"How about this? Tomorrow, I'll grab a few of my girlfriends, and we will meet you at the field. After, we can all go to Walter's and swim. Do you think he'd be cool with that?"

"Walter? He could care less. In fact, he'll love having people over. He's alone most of the time."

"That kinda sucks."

"Yeah, his dad's never around. When we get off the phone, I'll text him real quick to make sure it's ok. Then, I'll text you and let you know."

"Sounds good."

"Ok"

"Jeremy, before you go, I really think that you should do whatever your gut tells you to do. That's the best advice I can give you."

"Thanks, I appreciate that."

"Ok, so you'll text me later when you hear back from Walter?"

"Yes, I will."

129

"Ok, sounds like a plan. Talk to you later."

Jeremy touches the screen on his phone to end the call. He has made up his mind that tomorrow will be the day that he talks to the guys about St. Michael's. He did not know know how interesting the day will actually be.

11

The next morning at practice, there is a new kid standing on the sideline all by himself. He isn't too tall, but not that short either. He is really slim and his bright orange T-shirt makes him stand out from the other boys. Jeremy notices that no one is talking to him, so he decides to walk over and meet the new kid. "Hey, what's up? My name's Jeremy, but everybody calls me 'Savvy' because my last name is Savage. What's your name?"

The kid looks Jeremy up and down. "The name is Carlos Martinez, but people back home all call me 'Los.'"

"Ok, 'Los. Where you from?"

"Little bit of everywhere. Last year I lived in Florida. My dad's in the Navy and gets moved around a lot. He just got stationed up here a few weeks ago. It took me a while to find the team."

"Did you play football least year?"

"Yeah. I was a freshman last year and started at running back on JV. What position do you play?"

"Quarterback."

"Figures. Well, I guess it's good to get to know the guy that's going to be handing me the rock all the time."

"Oh yeah? You any good?"

Carlos smiles widely, "I'm the slipperiest thing you've ever seen in your life. Can't nobody catch me." He then pretends like he is juking and spinning past defenders.

"Good, because we can really use a running back with some speed."

"Well, look no further, my friend, because I am here!" The two continue talking for a while until the captains call for the start of practice.

"Hey Los, after practice I'll introduce you to the guys. You busy later?"

"No, why?"

"Good. See that dude right there?"

"The chubby one?"

"Easy man, that's my friend. But yeah, that one."

"Yeah, I see him."

"We are going to go to his house to hang out in the pool after practice. My girlfriend is bringing some of her friends, too. It'll be fun."

"Sounds good to me. First day here and I get football and a pool party; I can get used to this."

Practice starts with the usual break-up into offense and defense. Daniel notices that Jeremy is walking towards him with someone he has never seen before. He speaks to Sean, "Hey, you know who that is?"

Sean tightens up one of the laces on his cleats. "Yeah, that's the new kid. I think his name is Carlo, Carlos, or something like that. I hear he's got some speed."

"Good, let's see what he's got."

Sean and Daniel get the offense together and start by having them walk through the plays. They decide quickly to step it up to full speed. "Ok, I need eleven guys to stand on the other side and act like the defense. Your job is simple; tag the offensive player with the ball as soon as you can. When that happens, the play is dead, and we start over from there." Sean selects eleven guys and positions them on the field. He looks at Carlos, "You ready to go? I want to see if you can play or not." Carlos nods, "Yeah, I'm always ready to go."

"Good, get in at running back. Daniel, you call the plays. I'll take care of the defensive side."

The offense huddles around Daniel. "Carlos, is it? You're up. I need to get an idea of what I'm working with. We're going simple; pitch right on two, pitch right on two. Ready, go"

The offense lines up and gets ready to run the play. The ball is hiked back to Jeremy who quickly turns to his right and pitches the ball to the streaking Carlos. Carlos takes hold of the ball and tucks it under his arm. He makes a quick stutter step and blows past one defender. He spins past two more and easily accelerates past everyone as he hits the open field.

Carlos runs the ball back in to the huddle and flips it to the center, who then spots it on the ground. Jeremy gives Carolos a high five. "You weren't kidding; you've got some wheels."

"What did I say to you? I'm slick out there."

Daniel looks fairly impressed, "Not bad, kid. Now that they know what you can do, let's see if you can do it again. Toss left on one, toss left on one. Ready, go."

The offense lines up. Jeremy checks over his shoulder to Carlos who winks back at him. The ball is snapped, and Jeremy tosses it perfectly to the surging Carlos. This time, two defenders have him completely lined up. Carlos stops, takes a jab step back, then redirects his body effortlessly to his left, leaving the defenders grasping at nothing but air. He rounds the corner and turns on the jets. No one has any chance of keeping up with him as he streaks down the field.

For a second time, he jogs back to the huddle and flips the ball to the center. "Too easy baby; it's just too easy. I'm not even gassing it yet. Wait till you see what happens when I do that!"

Practice continues for the next hour with Jeremy, Ricky, and Carlos dazzling the other guys on offense. Carlos can not only run, he can catch too. It is an incredible advantage to have a running back that has great hands out of the backfield to go along with break neck speed. He is a virtual super weapon. When you line up Carlos next to Ricky, it is nearly impossible for opposing defenses to match-up with them.

Jeremy can see Lauren with a few of her girlfriends in the stands. She is rooting him on from time to time but mostly talking with her friends. The team stops for a water break. Jeremy uses this opportunity to walk over to her. She hops off the bench and lands smoothly on the ground. Jeremy moves to give her a kiss on the cheek, but she backs up. Lauren says smiling, "Um, you're kinda sweaty right now; maybe later." Jeremy smirks, "Yeah, I guess I'm a little gross right now. What do you expect? It's hot out here!"

"The pool is going to feel nice after sitting in this sun for so long, but at least I'm getting a tan while I watch you guys. You're positive that Walter is ok with us coming with you guys, right?"

"Trust me. Walter's more than ok with it. I think he almost crapped himself when I said you were bringing girls to his pool."

A voice booms from behind Jeremy, "Hey Savvy! If you're done talking to your girlfriend, we'd like to continue with practice!" Jeremy doesn't have to turn around to know that it's Clifton speaking to him.

"I've got to get back. We will be done in like a half hour or so."

With that, Lauren climbs back to her seat, and Jeremy runs back onto the practice field.

"It's that time again: seven-on-seven. Offense over there; defense with me."

Daniel kneels down in the middle of the offensive huddle, "Let's see if we can get Carlos the ball right away. Trips right. Carlos, you're on the inside. As soon as Jeremy gets the ball, you're going to head to the sideline, then run straight upfield. Ricky and I are going to run post routes to free you up. Jeremy, get that ball out ahead of him and make him go and get it. Let's see just how fast he really is."

The ball is hiked back to Jeremy. He pats the ball once, then twice, and looks directly at the middle of the field. Out of the corner of his peripheral vision, he can see that Carlos has easily run past the defender.

Jeremy set his feet and quickly moves his body to line up his throw. The ball cruises out of Jeremy's hand and sails over forty yards in the air as it lands smoothly in Carlos' hands for an easy touchdown. Jeremy pumps his fist high in the air as Carlos jogs his way back to the huddle.

"Damn, Savvy. You've got an arm on you."

"Thanks. Way to get open."

Carlos laughs, "There ain't anyone over there that can keep up with this." Carlos flexes his diminutive muscles and then shuffles his feet like he is dancing.

As the drill continues, the defense is just not able to match the speed of both Carlos and Ricky. They try to key in on one, but the other gets open. They attempt to double both, but that leaves one-on-one coverage on the other receivers, which Jeremy easily picks apart. No matter what defense Clifton tries to set his side up in, the offense finds a way to move the ball and eventually score. This happens on every single drive. The only points the defense scores are on a handful of sacks, resulting in a heavily lopsided win for the offense.

Clifton gathers the team together, "Before I say anything else, I think we should all put our hands together for that incredible display the offense put on for all of us today." The team claps loudly as Zach and Larry pat Jeremy on the back through the noise. Clifton continues, "I'm not proud to say that we, as a defense, got completely embarrassed out there, but we did. We have a lot to work on. However, I'd like to say that I am personally very happy that our new teammate, Carlos, is on *this* team. Carlos, wherever you are, you are not someone I want to play against this year, and I'm glad the only time I'll be going up against you, will be in practice." Jeremy and the other guys surrounding Carlos cheer him on as he steps forward and takes a bow.

"Thanks! I'd just like to say that I'm glad to be here, and that I'm looking forward to having you all as teammates this year," says Carlos. "Everyone here had been really cool to me so far, and I just want to say thanks for being so welcoming to the new kid."

Once Carlos is finished speaking, Clifton continues, "As I said, Defense, we've got a lot of work to do. Offense, you look like you're ready to take this team to the next level. I'll see you all here tomorrow for practice."

Jeremy, Carlos, Ricky, Jeff, Walter, Zach, and Larry walk over to the group of girls sitting in the stands. Lauren hops down and slowly struts up to Walter. "Walter, thanks so much for letting us come over today and use your pool. You're sure it's ok, right?"

"Yeah, I already told Jeremy it's no problem at all. My dad's never home and as long as I'm not throwing some sort of a party, he couldn't care less what I do."

"Great, as I'm sure you can tell, I brought some of my friends along with me to hang out at your house."

To no one's surprise, Larry is already in the middle of the girls, making the whole group laugh.

"Yeah, your friends can all come; it's really no biggie at all. We can order pizza or something when we get there. It's only about a ten minute walk from here," said Walter.

"Great!" Lauren takes a few steps over and stands next to Jeremy. "You looked pretty good out there QB. Nice job throwing that ball around. I mean, you definitely missed a few guys that were wide open, but, hey, no one's perfect."

"Jeez, thanks."

"Well, wouldn't you rather me be honest?"

"I suppose. As long as you don't beat me up too bad."

"Don't miss any open guys. This way I won't have to tell you about it."

The more Jeremy gets to know Lauren, the more he likes her. She isn't like the typical girl that he usually hangs out with. Those girls toss their hair around and tell him how great he is. Lauren is brutally

138

honest, a quality that he loves, and she doesn't mince words. If she has something to say, you will know about it. If you do something that she doesn't like, she has no problems telling you about it. She is beautiful, smart, and confident. Jeremy can't be sure of it, he has never loved anyone other than a relative before, but he thinks that he may be falling for her.

12

The group walks together towards Walter's house. As they do, Jeremy and Lauren, holding hands, find themselves at the back of the pack. "So, have you said anything to the guys about St. Michael's yet?"

"No."

"Chicken!"

"It's not that. I just wanted to wait till after practice. I'm going to talk to them at Walter's."

"I was just kidding; I know this is going to be difficult. It's pretty obvious that these guys mean a lot to you."

"Yeah, but it's not just that. Did you see Carlos out there today? That kid can really play. And Clifton is one of the most intense guys I've ever seen. He's going to do whatever it takes to win. Centerville may be better this year than people think they will."

"They definitely will be, if you play there."

"Thanks for that. Why don't you make this even harder for me? Seriously, though, after these last few days, I've been getting the feeling that this may be something I want to be a part of."

Lauren smiles and gives him a quick kiss. "Yuck! Your lips are salty!" She makes a funny face and wipes her mouth. "Anyway, I really hope you choose to stay, but I think I'll keep you around either way."

The group continues to walk until they reach the gigantic dwelling that Walter calls his house. Lauren stops dead in her tracks. "Wow! This is his house?"

Jeremy can't help but laugh. This is the typical reaction everyone has the first time they see Walter's place. "Yeah, this is it. Not too bad, huh?" Standing a few feet in front of them still gawking at the house, is Carlos. On Jeremy's way by, he nudges Carlos lightly in the ribs, "You coming or what Los?" Carlos excitedly jumps up and down. "It's like I won the lottery or something! This is going to be great!"

The house sits a few hundred feet back from the street, partially hidden from view, thanks to the soaring cherry trees which stand proudly at various spots on the property. During the winter, all of the leaves of these beautiful trees are gone, allowing passerbys to see the expansive home more clearly. However, during the spring and summer, the leaves are in full bloom, nearly completely obscuring the house from street view.

The home is constructed of all brick, with intricate roof angles that accentuate the supreme craftsmanship of the dwelling. Most impressively, it sits on an incredible twenty acres of land which borders a nearby stream. Walter's father spared no expense and flew in his own special contractor and workers that he had used on previous out-of-state projects. He hired special architects from New York City to help craft the most remarkable home anyone in Centerville had ever seen. To call the home a modern miracle would be a vast understatement. It is exceptional in every facet of its construction and design, right down to the most minute detail.

Carlos runs and catches up to Jeremy. "This place is crazy!" Jeremy smirks, "Wait till you see the backyard."

The group enters the house. Lauren's friends gawk at not only the sheer size, but the incredible beauty of the interior. They pass through the kitchen and head out to the backyard.

The backyard is separated into four sections, which are connected seamlessly through exquisite design and intricate detail.

The first section displays a beautiful stone patio, which is covered by an extension of the rear roof line. This area features custom stone built-ins for the grill, refrigerator, trash, and a sink. The counter top is comprised of three-inch-thick limestone, which had to be shipped into Centerville from out of state.

A short set of steps leads you to a second section, which also features the same stone as the first. However, this section has a complete outdoor fireplace which is surrounded by two full-sized couches and a loveseat. To the right and left of the fireplace are two massive outdoor flat screen televisions which are currently featuring Walter's favorite action movie. Directly to the left of this area is probably the most astonishing of the four sections. Featured here is a custom-designed pool which was made to resemble a lagoon Walter's dad had seen once on vacation in Scotland. The backside of the pool is made to look like it has been carved into pure stone. There is a waterfall

142

which spumes water effortlessly down the stone face into the pool. There is also a diving board in the deep end of the pool, which is accompanied by twin water slides. The slides snake around before they eventually dump the rider into the pool.

On the right side of the pool is a ten-person hot tub, which flows water seamlessly from the tub into the pool. The fourth and final section of the yard is a large swath of meticulously maintained lawn. The lawn is surrounded by endless rows of mature trees. This section of the grounds features a full-sized sand volleyball court, full-sized basketball court, and complete batting cage. In totality, it is unlike anything most people will ever see, unless they are at a very high-priced resort.

Zach takes off at full speed and jumps into the water, fully clothed. Larry and Ricky follow closely behind. Next up is Carlos, who follows Zach's lead and jumps in with all of his football gear on, except for his sneakers.

Walter faces Lauren and her friends. "Excuse my Neanderthal friends. There are a number of bathrooms in the house. Please, use any one that you find to get changed. You guys can leave your stuff wherever you want. No one else is going to be here except for us."

The girls thank Walter and walk back into the house to change. Lauren squeezes Jeremy's hand, "You may want to use this opportunity to talk to the guys before the girls come out and distract them."

"You're probably right."

"Of course I am." She gives Jeremy's hand another squeeze and walks into the house.

Jeremy drags his feet over to the pool where the guys are taking turns splashing each other in the face. "Hey guys, do you mind if I talk to you all for a second?" Zach rocks his arm back and sends it rifling through the water creating a massive surge in Larry's direction. The wave makes contact with Larry's skin, sending cresting water crashing into his face. "You wait! I'm going to get you back for that one."

Jeremy repeats himself, this time a little louder. The guys stop messing around and swim their way to the edge of the pool closest to him.

"There's something I've wanted to talk to you guys about, but I haven't found the right time for it. I guess, now's as good as I'm going to get." Jeremy inhales and exhales deeply then continues, "There are two things I want to tell you guys. First, I won't be around next week because I'm going to this football camp in California. Second, I've been offered a chance to play at St. Michael's next year."

The pool falls completely silent as Jeremy carries on, "I haven't made up my mind if I want to play at Centerville or St. Michael's just yet. You guys are my best friends in the world, and I want to talk to you all before I make my final decision."

Carlos is the first to speak as the other guys stand there motionless, "I only just met all of you, but I really hope you choose to play at Centerville, Savvy. I mean, I thought that we, as an offense, had

144

really good chemistry out there today. I've played on a number of teams in the past, and I feel like this one's got some good stuff happening on it."

Ricky is next, "I've also gotten an offer to play at St. Michael's."

Zach looks stunned while Larry, Jeff, and Walter are still completely speechless. On Zach's face is a mixture of shock as well as confusion. "I don't understand. You're not going to go to Centerville next year? Neither of you?" The look on Zach's face slices right through Jeremy's heart. It is a look of complete betrayal.

"I never said that," says Jeremy. "I need to decide soon what I'm going to do. But, I wanted to talk to you guys first before I make any decisions."

Walter finds his voice, "What did your parents say?"

"They said it was up to me, but that St. Michael's has more to offer than Centerville." Zach turns to face Ricky, "And you?"

"I'm pretty positive that I'm going to go to St. Michael's. I've been waiting for this opportunity." Zach just stands there, in the middle of the pool, shaking his head. "I thought we were a family. I thought that we were going to stick together, no matter what. We've been playing football together since we were little. Doesn't that count for something?"

Jeremy's stomach continues to sink. He feels about two inches tall. He is sitting here, trying to talk to Zach and his other friends about

145

abandoning them. Zach, the guy that jumped into a fight to save him just the other night. Zach's face still exudes the emotions he is currently feeling. It is a mixture of complete disbelief and hurt. "Well, if you want my opinion, I think that it would suck if you two went somewhere else," said Zach.

"I know I don't know you two like these guys do, but the little I do know of you guys, I like, and I'd like the chance to get to know you better. Plus after practicing with you both today, I definitely would like to play on the same team," said Carlos.

Jeremy looks at Larry, "What about you?"

Larry takes the time to collect his thoughts before responding, "You know, I want to keep doing the same stuff we've been doing for years. I want to play on the same team and hang out just like we're doing now, all throughout high school. But, if you guys think that going to St. Michael's is really the best thing for you both, then I think you need to do what you feel is best for your future. Do I want to lose our two best offensive weapons? Obviously not; but, I'm not going to get in the way, either."

Walter sits there quietly listening to his friends talk and says nothing. Jeremy moves a step closer to him. "What do you think, Walter?"

"I think that you should go to Centerville for a number of reasons, some of which, I'll admit, are pretty selfish of me. I like hanging out with you, and I want that to continue. I don't know

146

everything there is to know about St. Michael's, but I do know that they are basically good at everything. At Centerville, you will be the center of attention. More importantly, I think that if you take a team like Centerville to a state title, then you've really proven how great you are.

Taking St. Michael's to another title is one thing, but taking a team that has never won even one championship in its history to a title; that's legendary. That's the kind of stuff that gets talked about for years and years after you graduate."

Jeremy had not looked at it from that angle before. The main reason for him to stay and play in Centerville was really to be with his friends. But now, Walter has made possibly the best argument for him to play for Centerville High. He can go to St. Michael's and be good, but the team is already really good. A true challenge is to take a team like Centerville and bring them to new heights. Besides, this new kid Carlos can really run and with Zach and Clifton on defense, they may be able to really surprise some people.

"You know what, Walter? I haven't looked at it that way before. You've definitely given me something new to think about."

The discussion abruptly comes to a halt as the girls strut out of the house and over to the pool. As they walk towards them, Carlos can't help but stare. Every girl that comes out of the house looks like a perfect ten to him. He plunges his head under the water and wipes his eyes, half expecting to see something different than what he thought he

147

saw. Needless to say, he is pleasantly surprised to find out that, as they get closer, they are even prettier than he thought they were.

Zach storms up the stairs leading out of the pool and rips off his shirt. He throws it on the ground and flops his body down onto a lounge chair. Lauren comes over to Jeremy and wraps an arm around his waist, "How'd it go?"

"Not as bad as I thought, but I think Zach is pretty peeved."

"Did it help you to make up your mind?"

"Actually, thanks to something Walter said, it made it even more complicated."

She rested her head on his shoulder. "Good luck with that."

13

"Jess, you ready to go or what?"

Jessica is frantically running around the bedroom trying in vain to find just the right combination of clothing and accessories fit for their meeting with the mayor.

David's voice echoes loudly throughout the house, "We need to get going if we are going to get there on time."

"I know that, Dear. You said you talked to Jeremy, and he's going to Walter's after practice, right?"

"Yeah. All the boys are going to Walter's house after practice. Are you almost done up there or what?"

Jessica finally feels as though she has the right outfit on. She gives herself one last look in the mirror. She re-tucks her white blouse into her long black skirt and adjusts her earrings one more time.

On her way out the door, she flips her hand and snaps off the light. She comes down the steps, and David lets out a loud whistle. "You look beautiful, Honey." He gives her a kiss on the forehead and then checks his watch for the fourth time in the last hour. "But, we really need to get out of here."

"I know, I know. I'm ready." She looks around the kitchen for one last check, and follows David out the door.

The two get into the car and wait for the garage door to open. David turns to face her, "So, what do you think the mayor wants to discuss with us?"

Jessica really has absolutely no clue. The woman on the phone hadn't given her any information at all that would help her figure out what this was all about. "I have no idea David, but it must be something pretty important if he is willing to take time out of his busy schedule to meet with us. Why else would a man with a crazy, hectic schedule like the mayor find the time to sit with us?"

They drive to the town's administration building and find a parking spot. David presses the alarm button on the keypad and locks the doors to the car. They walk up to the front and pull open the large wooden doors. David checks his watch yet again; the time reads: 11:58 A.M.

The receptionist greets them cheerily, "Hello, my name is Tami. How may I help you?"

David takes a step forward, "Hello. I'm David Savage, and this is my wife, Jessica. We have a meeting with the mayor at twelve."

"Oh, yes. I was told that you were coming. Please, have a seat. I'll tell Courtney that you are here. She's been expecting you."

The woman taps a button on her phone and speaks into the receiver for only a few seconds. Minutes later a young, attractive woman, probably in her late twenties, emerges from an office door. She

150

strides up confidently to David and Jessica, "Hello, Mr. and Mrs. Savage. It's a pleasure to meet you both. The mayor is ready for you."

The young woman leads the way through a beautifully polished oak wood door and down a long corridor. The hallway opens up to a waiting room. At the end of the waiting room, stands another door. Courtney motions for David and Jessica to follow her as she softly knocks on the door.

"Come in," sounds from within.

Courtney opens the door and waits while David and Jessica enter the room.

"Mr. Mayor, Mr. and Mrs. Savage are here to see you."

"Thank you, Courtney." Courtney smiles in the direction of David and Jessica and closes the door behind her.

Mayor Clinton Thompson stands up from his seat. Although he is in his early fifties, he looks much younger than his age. He is trim, yet stocky, with large shoulders and chiseled features. His hair, a blend of black and grey, sits well-manicured and perfectly trimmed upon his head. The black suit he dons is tailored with precision, and his spotless white shirt is pressed to perfection. His tie, a light shade of silver, is also flattened and straightened to excellence. David and Jessica have seen him numerous times before on television during election years and have never once seen him look anything short of perfect.

He takes a few strides around his desk and proffers his hand towards Jessica. She accepts it and shakes his hand gently. "So nice to meet you, Mrs. Savage." He then turns his attention to David, "Hello, Mr. Savage. It's a pleasure to meet you as well." The mayor motions for them to sit in the two seats directly in front of his desk, "Please, have a seat." David and Jessica sit down as he makes his way back around his desk and sits.

"Well, I bet you two are wondering why I asked you to meet with me." Jessica smiles nervously and looks at David. David says, "Yes, we truly have no idea why you'd be interested in meeting with us regarding our son."

The mayor claps his hands together loudly, "Yes, your son Jeremy. I've heard many incredible things about your boy. To tell you a little secret, I was actually at the Junior League championship game and watched him win it for Centerville. You wouldn't have noticed me; I kept myself pretty covered up so as not to attract any attention. Anyway, he has a really special talent."

This time, Jessica speaks, "Why, thank you, Mr. Mayor. We have been hearing a lot of that lately."

"And that is precisely why I wanted to meet with you. I know that Jeremy will, and most likely already has, received multiple offers to go to schools other than Centerville High. There's little doubt in my mind that St. Michael's has already contacted you. Am I right?"

"Actually, Coach Fletcher was at our house yesterday," said David.

The mayor shakes his head violently, showing his displeasure with the news, "I knew it. Every time Centerville produces something, St. Michael's comes in and tries to take it away from us. They're usually successful at it, too. But, I would like you two to consider something for me."

"That would be?" asks Jessica.

"Allowing Jeremy to attend Centerville High School in the fall. I know what you're thinking, why on Earth would the mayor of the town invite us here just to listen to him lobby for our son to attend the local high school? Truth is, this is something near and dear to my heart. See, I love football. I have all my life. More than that, I love this town. As you probably know, I've lived here my whole life. My great-grandparents were some of the first to live in Centerville, and the Thompson's have never left. I have a great deal of pride in our little town."

David looks a little confused, "We love it here in Centerville as well, but I still don't quite understand why we are here."

The mayor leans back in his chair, "I'm glad you both love this town, too. See, Jeremy is a special kind of football player. The kind that doesn't come around too often. He is also the kind that can take a struggling football team such as Centerville's, and lead it to out of the gutter, so to speak." His voice lowers a bit as he continues, "Let me tell you, there are a lot of very important people in this town that would love to see Centerville on the big stage. In fact, a small group of us have

153

elected to extend a special invitation to the two of you. We would appreciate it if you would both join us for dinner tonight at the Pemberton Country Club."

Pemberton Country Club is the most exclusive golf and social club in Centerville. The waiting list is over a mile long, and its membership boasts not only the mayor, but two congressmen, a senator, and other members of Centerville's elite class. David has always wanted to play there, but has not been able to find anyone that could get him access.

Jessica's heart is racing. Only the highest of the high go to events at Pemberton. Before David can say anything, she excitedly says, "We would love to go!" David, seeing the look of pure exhilaration on his wife's face, simply nods in agreement.

"Fantastic! You are both going to love it there. Dinner will be at seven, drinks start at six. Please, come as early as you'd like. As a matter of fact, David, how about you and I play 18 tomorrow morning?"

"Wow, really? That would be incredible; I've never played there before, but I've always wanted to."

"Really? Well, that won't be a problem for you anymore; you can play anytime you'd like."

David scratches his head, "Pemberton is members only, correct?"

"Of course it is, and you two are its newest members. Don't worry about the membership fees or anything like that. It's all been taken care of already. Jessica, I have something here that I think you will like as well." The mayor opens a drawer in his desk and takes out a white envelope. He offers it to Jessica, "Here, these are for you. I had a feeling that David might enjoy the golfing, so I wanted to make sure I had a little something for you as well."

Jessica takes the envelope from his hand and unseals it. Inside are two tickets to her favorite show, which will be performing soon on Broadway.

"I love this show! Oh, this is too generous of you! Thank you so much!"

"I'm happy to hear it's a show that you like. I took a guess at it. Did you happen to notice where the seats are?" Jessica's eyes quickly scan over the ticket, which depicts the name of the show, the night, and time. She keeps looking and then she sees it. "Oh my goodness!" She turns to face David, "David, these are front row tickets! This is incredible!" She looks to the mayor, "I can't believe this! These tickets are so hard to get and front row, no less!" Her excitement bleeds into every word as she clutches the envelope for dear life. "Truly, Mr. Mayor, thank you so much for these." Jessica loves the tickets, as well as the invitation to the club, but she can feel something inside of her compelling her to say something. "Mr. Mayor, the tickets and the country club are wonderful, but I feel like I need to say something to

155

you. We can't accept these gifts if you think that it means that Jeremy is going to go to Centerville. We are letting him make up his own mind on that."

The mayor shifts nervously in his seat. This is a conversation he was hoping to avoid. "I fully understand that Jeremy will be the one making this decision. These gifts are simply to demonstrate to both of you how committed I am to you and your family. No strings attached, I promise. Look, I'm just happy I picked a show that you like." The mayor punches a button in his phone. "Yes, Mr. Mayor?"

"Courtney, would you mind coming in here and showing Mr. and Mrs. Savage out please?'

"Right away, sir."

The mayor stands up from behind his desk and escorts them to the door. "I'm sorry to end our meeting abruptly like this, but I have a pretty busy schedule for the rest of the day. I'm really looking forward to tonight. I think you two are going to enjoy some of the things we have to say." The mayor shakes both of their hands again, and Courtney leads them out of the office.

The mayor waits until the door is closed and picks up his phone. He dials the number he has used countless times and waits for the person on the other end to pick up.

A voice sounds from the other end, "I assume the gifts were well-received?"

"You have done very well once again. The tickets were a complete success, and the Pemberton membership seems to also be a hit with both of them. Have you been able to find anything else I can use?"

"Not much, they are both squeaky clean. The woman, Jessica, likes to be pampered. You and your friends should be able to use that to your advantage. The husband has very few hobbies. He's into sports, perhaps tickets to a baseball or football game with VIP treatment, have him meet some current stars on the teams; things like that are your best bet to get in his good graces."

"Thank you. That gives me a few ideas to work with. I'll call again if I need anything else. I'm guessing you already received my payment?"

"Yes, it was wired into my account two days ago."

"Excellent." The mayor ends the call and relaxes in his chair.

"It was a delight to meet you both. I hope to see you again sometime soon." With that, Courtney turns and disappears back through the door they had just exited.

Jessica can't contain her excitement as she thrusts herself into her car seat. "Can you believe that? We are going to Pemberton tonight! I've always wanted to go there for something."

David turns to his wife. "I can't believe they were able to make us members, just like that: no waiting list, no fees, no nothing."

Jessica smiles brightly, "David, they are the cream of the crop. Money is no object to them. Can you believe he got me those tickets?

And tonight, we are going to get wined and dined by them. You do know what's happening, right?'

David puts the key in the ignition and starts the engine. "It seems that there are a few people that really want our son to go to Centerville. But, I thought that you and I were in agreement that St. Michael's was the best place for Jeremy."

"Well, maybe we were a little too hasty in simply brushing off Centerville. Besides, it really seems like Jeremy is leaning towards Centerville anyway. We did say that we were going to let him make his own decision. However, if there are some things discussed tonight that we like, then perhaps we start to move away from St. Michael's and begin to see the full benefits of Centerville High."

David turns the car out of the parking lot and out onto the main road. Thoughts race through his mind about what, exactly, is going to happen tonight. He and Jeremy are leaving very soon to go to California for the sports camp. A decision is going to have to be made shortly. He just can't believe it. He, the middle school teacher, is now a member at Pemberton.

They arrive back at home. Jessica bursts through the door and heads directly upstairs where she rifles through her already picked apart closet. She whips out a hanger with a dress on it and spins it around in her hand. "Nah, not nice enough." She places it back and continues her search.

By the time David gets upstairs, there is no part of the bed that can be seen. Hangers, dresses, shirts, skirts, and shoes are littered all over the place. His wife is looking at herself in the mirror and doesn't even notice that he has walked in.

"That one looks nice on you." She turns around and makes a face. Unsatisfied with the dress, she walks back into the closet and continues looking. She emerges with a different dress on; this one David *really* likes.

"Wow, you look incredible in that." She saunters over to the mirror. She turns from this way to that, making sure to check out every angle of the way she looks in the dress. She steps back and continues to fidget. She finds a pair of shoes in the chaos on the bed and steps into them. She tucks her hair behind her ears and takes a long look. She makes a strange sound and then kicks off the shoes, sending them flying in the direction of the closet. She searches for, and finds, a different pair of shoes and positions herself in front of the mirror again.

Having been married for quite a while now, David knows to stay quiet during this process. He has learned to only give positive feedback when she asks for his thoughts. He watches for a few more moments, then, making no noise, slowly walks into the closet. He takes out the suit he knows he is going to wear. He unwraps it from the plastic and attempts to lay it out on the bed. Noticing there is absolutely no room, he turns around and hangs it back up on his side of the closet. He

159

reappears from out of the closet and finds that Jessica is waiting for him.

"What do you think of this?"

"You look stunning in that dress."

"You always say stuff like that. Seriously, what do you think? Is this Pemberton material?"

David steps towards his wife and places his hands on her hips. "You are the most beautiful woman I have ever seen. I thought that almost twenty years ago, and I still feel that way today. In this dress, you shine. I'm just worried that I may not be able to measure up."

She smiles and gives him a soft kiss. "Are you wearing that grey suit that I love?"

"Yes, I am."

"And are you going to wear it with the stripped black tie that I bought for you?"

"Absolutely. Already took the suit out of the plastic and have the tie hanging on the hanger."

She leans in and gives him another kiss. "Then, I think you will look dashing. What time is it now?"

David checks his watch, "It's 1:45."

"Good, we have enough time to eat some lunch and relax a bit before tonight. And I should also have plenty of time to shower, do my hair, and get ready. You know my process; it's about an hour for me to get ready, practically to the second." David chortles, "Yes, dear. I know."

"Would you mind texting or calling Jeremy and letting him know that we are going to be out tonight? See if he can stay at Zach's or one of the others boys' houses tonight; I don't want to feel rushed. I'm going to clean up this mess I made and then make lunch."

David takes his phone out of his pocket and swipes his thumb across the screen, bringing the phone to life. He thumbs through his contacts until he finds Jeremy. He sends him a short text message. Jeremy quickly responds saying that he is at Walter's house now with all the guys and is going to stay at Walter's for a while then head over to Zach's.

"All set, Jess. He's at Walter's now and is going to stay there for a while. Later, he's either going to just stay there or head over to Zach's."

"Perfect!" came her response. David walks down the stairs, takes a seat on the couch, and turns on the television.

14

A few hours later, David and Jessica arrive at Pemberton Country Club. David pulls the car up to the front door. A valet quickly jogs out of the entrance and opens Jessica's door. "Welcome to Pemberton Country Club, mam." Jessica gets out of the car and waits for David to join her. David gives the keys to the valet, who then hands him a ticket. "When you two are finished for the evening, just hand that ticket to any of our valets, and we will promptly retrieve your car."

David walks around the car and extends his elbow towards Jessica. She wraps her arm around it. Together, they walk towards the front door. As they approach, the doors whisk open. They are held in place by two gentlemen in very formal-looking attire, who smile politely and greet them both.

David and Jessica enter the main lobby and look at each other. The foyer of the country club is gorgeous. Ornate woodwork and beautiful artwork exude the elegance of the exclusive club. The hardwood floor gleams brightly as they stroll across it. They take a few more steps and are greeted by a woman in a black suit, who is wearing white gloves. "Mr. and Mrs. Savage, I presume?"

Jessica nods, "Yes, that's us."

"Please, would you be so kind as to follow me this way?" The woman waves a white-gloved hand to her right and then begins to walk. She comes to a large set of double-doors and opens the left side. She smoothly slides her back and hips to the door, securing it open and extends a hand. "There are a few members of your party that are already here. Please, enjoy cocktails at the bar. Hors d'oeuvres will be passed in fifteen minutes."

David and Jessica thank her and enter the room. The room looks a lot like other ballrooms they have been in for weddings or events. Except this one is far larger and has been exquisitely taken care of. As they gaze around the room taking in the splendor of all that they see, neither one can find a single thing that appears to be out of place. Everything about the room is perfect, right down to the crisp folds in the napkins, which are resting on the table.

There are four men and three women already standing by the bar having cocktails. They are engaging in a discussion; one of the men is talking animatedly, gesturing wildly with his hands. He spills some of the contents of his drink to the floor as he continues to gesticulate. Seemingly out of nowhere, a woman suddenly appears to clean the mess. She is gone almost as fast as she arrived.

As the door shuts behind David and Jessica, it makes a low noise, but audible enough to attract the attention of those already in attendance. Upon seeing them, one member of the group beckons to David and Jessica to join.

David and Jessica join the group. One by one, they each step forward and introduce themselves. Every person seems to go out of their way to say what an honor it is to meet David and Jessica. They

163

also mention how they have heard many great things about their son, the football star. It is so seamless that it's almost as if the whole thing has been rehearsed a number of times before David and Jessica arrived.

Within a half-hour, the other participants have arrived. The mayor is the last to show up, apologizing to everyone for being late. Apparently, he had been held up by some last minute financial work that simply couldn't wait. He makes his way around the room, shaking hands as he passes through the small gathering. He eventually winds up in front of Jeremy's parents. "I'm so glad you two decided to join us this evening. I hope that my friends here haven't treated you too poorly in my absence."

"Not at all," David responds. "Quite the contrary, everyone has been exceptionally gracious to us."

"Good, I'm glad to hear it." The mayor wraps his arms around the shoulders of two gentlemen standing on either side of him. "You know, some of the people here think that they are big shots or something, so I'm glad you two have enjoyed yourselves this far." The two men laugh as the mayor releases his arms.

Through conversation, David and Jessica learn that the two men are actually brothers, which seems odd because they look nothing alike. Their family has had members at Pemberton for three generations. They are real estate developers and are quite profitable. It also comes to light that the two of them have donated a sizeable amount to not only the mayor's campaign, but also to a few select congressmen's, who are also both present this evening.

Jessica struggles to contain her zeal for this lifestyle. She absolutely loves every second of everything that has happened thus far. The food is incredible, the service impeccable, and the company is the most exclusive and interesting in all of Centerville. She feels like royalty.

David is enjoying himself, as well, but not to the same extent as his wife, who has drifted off with some of the other ladies at the dinner party. Deep down, he feels a little out of place, hob knobbing with the upper class, but he does have an appreciation for superb food and superior wine, which are in abundance at Pemberton, and they haven't even gotten to the dinner yet.

The mayor, the two brothers, and another gentleman, Clyde Rainsworth, surround David. The mayor takes a step forward. "David, before we get to dinner, which is going to be incredible by the way, we wanted to speak to you about your son." He looks to the men surrounding David and continues, "All of us here have a love for Centerville. We want to see it flourish. It is in all of our collective best interests that Centerville be as successful as it can be. A major part of that is tied to our school system."

All of the men nod in agreement. The mayor continues, "Did you know that prep schools, like St. Michael's, have been poaching our best and brightest for years? They come in, take our most talented

165

athletes and our brightest students, and then leave. This is something that we, as a group, want to stop."

One of the brothers takes a sip from his drink and picks up where the mayor left off, "If our schools can thrive and produce students that go on to Division I athletic programs and attend Ivy League schools, it will bode very well for us as a community."

David is struggling to see the connection the men are trying to make. Acknowledging this, the man named Clyde speaks up, "What my friends are trying so eloquently to say is that the better products we graduate; the higher up the ladder our town can climb. Your son, by himself, can put our football program on the map. If he decides to go to Centerville, maybe other students would consider staying, as opposed to immediately electing to go to schools like St. Michael's. Furthermore, if we begin to build a reputation as a dominant school, more people will want to come here to live because we have a better school system. This means more residents, which in turn, will drive up real estate prices, and will mean more jobs and so on and so on."

The mayor waits patiently for Clyde to finish and starts up again, "You have to understand, David, it has to start with someone. It can't just be someone on a small scale either, but someone major that can really elicit the type of shift we are talking about. Your son provides such an opportunity. He can be the one that begins to turn the tide in our favor and helps us to take Centerville to a whole new level."

166

David stands there listening to all that the men have to say. The more they talk, the more he realizes that they are right. Why should schools like St. Michael's always take the best from his town? Why shouldn't Centerville High get to keep its best and brightest? He starts to succumb to the notion that his son can be a pioneer for this town. He can become so much more than an incredible football player if he went to Centerville. He can become a local hero.

"I completely agree with what you gentlemen are saying, and I definitely see your points. My wife and I are ultimately going to let Jeremy make up his own mind; however, since you've brought something new to the table, something we've never even considered, I think it's important that Jeremy understand what he means to the town already and how much more he could eventually mean to this town. He needs to know how important he truly is to Centerville."

The men around David all smile at each other. "We can't tell you how happy we are that you're on board," says the mayor. "We understand that Jeremy isn't a child anymore and should make his own choices. We simply ask that he be well-informed before making this critical life choice. We know that St. Michael's comes to parents like you and boasts about their achievements. That's not lost on us; however, I can assure you that if Jeremy elects to attend Centerville High, we will make sure that his choice is richly rewarded. Consider the membership here as just a sample of what awaits you in the future."

On the other side of the room, Jessica is taking the time to savor every moment of the evening. All of the women are being exceptionally nice to her. They tell her how beautiful she is, which of course, she doesn't mind, and how they would love to have her and David over for dinner. One woman looks at her, "Jessica, you really must come here often now that you and David are members. My husband and I try to dine here at least once or twice a week. I hope you two will do the same. I really look forward to getting to know you better in the future."

A second woman adds, "Yes, Jessica, you are going to love Pemberton. I'm not sure if you know this or not, but some of the ladies here try to get together once a month for spa day. We indulge in massages, manicures, pedicures, the works. It would be my pleasure if you would be my guest at the next spa day we have."

"Wow, that sounds incredible! Yes, of course, I'd love to join you at the next one."

"Splendid! As soon as I get the details, I'll be sure to fill you in. That reminds me, I need to get your number before the night is over."

"Oh, yes! Me too," says another woman.

"Me, as well!" exclaimed another.

The same woman that led Jessica and David to the room comes into view, "Attention everyone, if you would please take your seats, dinner is about to be served." The group walks over to the large table and takes their seats. On the plates in front of everyone is a small white notecard. On the notecard is the menu for this evening, listed in beautifully scripted font. David picks up the card and examines it. He turns to his wife, "This might be the best meal we ever eat in our lives, you know."

The group eats and drinks well into the evening. They share stories, jokes, and backgrounds. The chatter subsides, and the mayor uses this opportunity to stand up from his seat and raise his glass, "I'd like to make a toast to the guests of this evening. To David and Jessica. Thank you for joining us tonight. I hope the food and company were to your liking, and I look forward to seeing more of you both in the future. Salute!"

Everyone raises a glass and takes a sip of their drinks. Jessica elbows David sharply in the ribs, indicating that she would like him to say a few words in return. David stands up while Jessica smiles outwardly, "We would like to thank all of you for this evening. It has been an incredible experience. I don't think I've ever eaten that much before in my entire life! We'd also like to thank all of you for the wonderful things you have said about our son, Jeremy. It really does mean a lot to us. Finally, we'd also like to thank you for your interest in his future and for your passionate concern for the future of this town."

Less than an hour later, after dinner has finished being served, most members of the small gathering have vacated. The only ones still in attendance are David, Jessica, the mayor, and one other couple. David checks his watch and yawns, "Well, I almost hate to say it, but I really think we should be heading home soon. It's getting pretty late.

Besides, I'm sure this place would like to close. I'm surprised they haven't kicked us out already."

The mayor laughs, "I know for a fact they aren't going to kick this man out!" As he says that, he raises a glass towards a man standing next to him. David hadn't noticed him before and couldn't recall if he had been introduced to him or not that evening. David looks confusedly at the mayor. "I didn't introduce you two yet? My goodness, where are my manners? David Savage, meet Wilson Pemberton, owner of Pemberton Country Club."

David extends his hand, "It's a pleasure to meet you, Mr. Pemberton. You have an absolutely beautiful club here." The man firmly shakes David's hand, "Thank you very much, David. My family takes great pride in Pemberton. I heard from some of the members tonight that your boy is quite the football prodigy."

"Yes, sir, apparently he is."

"I'd love to meet him sometime." Wilson looks at his wife Eleanor, "Dear, when is the next time we are hosting juniors' night?"

She answers, "In two weeks, on Friday evening."

"David, why don't you have Jeremy come to juniors' night here at the club in two weeks? I'd love to have a chat with him. After, you and I can get to know each other better over a few rounds at the bar."

Eleanor listens and then faces Jessica, "While they do that, how about you and I have a night out on the town, my treat. I'll have my car meet us here. When your family arrives, our driver will take us wherever we want to go and bring us back later."

"That sounds amazing. I'd love to."

"Excellent! I haven't done that in quite some time. It should be fun! I will see you here at the club before that though, won't I?"

"Oh, I'm sure you will. We love it here. This place is absolutely stunning!"

David and Jessica say their goodbyes and head back towards the door, where one of the valets is waiting. "Hello, sir. Do you have your ticket?" David searches around in his pocket and pulls out his wallet. He opens it, retrieves his ticket, and hands it to the man. Seconds later, the man returns with their car. He quickly jumps out of the driver's seat and opens the passenger side door for Jessica. "Thank you" she says as she sits down. He walks over to the driver's side door and rests his hand on the door. David pulls out some money from his pocket for a tip and attempts to give it to the man, but he refuses to accept it. "No need, sir. Someone has already taken care of that."

"Who?"

"Mr. Thompson, sir."

David slides into the driver's side seat and grips the steering wheel. He pushes his foot down on the accelerator and heads towards home. Jessica is the first to speak, "Was that the best night of your life or what?"

"No, actually it was possibly the night we got married, or when our son was born, or…"

"You know what I mean! That was incredible! The place is magnificent, and everyone was so nice!"

David glances over at his wife while she continues to talk excitedly. He can't help but notice how happy she is. It made him feel good deep down to see her like that. After a little while, she finally takes a break. David uses this opportunity to speak, "You know, when I was talking to some of the men, they seemed really interested in Jeremy going to Centerville High."

"Really?"

"Yeah, they made some really good points, too. I think that on the flight to California, I'm going to have another talk with Jeremy. I want to make sure he knows some of the benefits of going to Centerville." David turns onto their street, the car eases down the road towards their house.

"I'm a little surprised at you. I thought that you were all in on St. Michael's."

David presses the garage door opener and watches as the door slowly moves up. "Well, the men I talked to tonight made some excellent points. They also said there could be some other perks to Jeremy going to Centerville." The door finishes opening, and David drives the car in. He puts the car in park and shuts off the engine.

"What does that mean?"

172

"I don't know; I didn't ask. But, they said that the free membership to Pemberton was just the tip of the iceberg and that there could be more heading our way if Jeremy goes to Centerville. I'm not saying that we should take a bunch of stuff, but if we get a few benefits out of Jeremy going to Centerville, which is where he may want to go anyway, then that works for me."

David opens the car door and slowly gets out. He takes a few steps towards the door and stops. "I realized something tonight, Jess."

"Oh yeah? What's that, Dear?" she says as she continues towards the door.

"If Jeremy really is as good as I think he will be, tonight is just a snapshot of the way our lives will be like from now on. People will want do things for us. They will pay for our dinners, buy us memberships to places, and take us wherever we want to go. The people that were there tonight were very, very interested in Jeremy going to Centerville. Can you imagine what it will be like when it's time for him to pick a college?"

Jessica says nothing in return. She merely concentrates on the notion of people kowtowing to her for the rest of her life, thanks to her son. She doesn't want to admit it, but she likes the thought of it. She likes being treated like she is someone special and receiving preferential treatment. It is nice for her to be doted on for a change and for her to have high-ranking friends that will bend over backwards to make her life and her family's life easier. The two of them walk through the door and up the stairs to bed without saying another word to each other.

15

The next morning, practice starts the same way it has for the previous four days. The captains guide the team through the usual stretching and warm-ups. Once that is finished, the team gathers together. This time Sean comes to the forefront, "Listen up, fellas; we have an announcement to make. Last night, we were contacted by another team to have a scrimmage today. I know that it's only been about a week since we started practices, but we feel that it will be a good challenge for us as a team. It will let us know where we stand with the better teams in the state."

Jeremy stares blankly at Zach and tries to figure out what team they could be playing. He then looks to Ricky who also seems to have no idea as to what is going on. He searches the faces of the rest of the guys on the team, but it appears that no one, except for the three captains has any idea what is about to happen.

Sean continues, "I'm sure right now you're all wondering what I'm talking about. Well, I'm talking about scrimmaging St. Michael's today, on this field, in exactly one hour." Murmuring can be heard throughout the team as the guys talk with one another and attempt to make sense of the announcement. Clifton raises his voice above the whispers, "Listen up! I'm tired of not getting any respect. I'm dead tired of people thinking that they can walk all over this team. You guys aren't stupid. You all know that Centerville hasn't done anything lately.

I don't think they've done anything since I've been alive, but all that means nothing. This is a new team, a completely different team, and we got something to say this year. We got talent! We got speed! We got heart, and we are a force to be reckoned with! This season really starts today, on this field. I know it's just a seven-on-seven scrimmage, but don't treat it like that. I want you to treat it like it's the last time you're ever going to set foot on a football field. I want you to play with the kind of heart that makes me proud to call you my teammates!"

Daniel jumps in, "Offense, we are going to get right into running plays to ensure we are ready for the challenge we are going to face today. Let's get to it."

Clifton speaks to the rest of the team, "Defense, today begins your quest to be the best. I'm asking that you give me everything you have. Every time we step on that field, I want you to know that I'm going to be giving every bit of myself to this team. All I ask in return is that you do the same. Follow my lead. Fight for the guy next to you. Fight for your teammates. If you do, then together we can't lose."

The team practices hard for the next hour or so. The summer sun shines relentlessly down upon them as sweat pours off the players. After a while, the captains call for a water break. As the players walk towards the coolers, two busses appear in the distance, kicking up clouds of dust as they drive down the dirt road to the field. The busses come to a stop on the grass a few feet away from where the team is standing. The doors open and streams of kids, all wearing the same

176

warm-up gear, flow off the busses. Once they are all off the busses, the team lines up in perfectly straight rows. The last to exit the bus is Coach Fletcher.

The coach treads confidently up to the captains of the Centerville team, "Hello, boys. My name is Coach Fletcher. My captains informed me this morning that they set up this little scrimmage with your team. So I decided, as a spectator only of course, to join the team and watch the game. As I'm sure you know, coaches can't have any interaction with players yet. I won't be on the sideline or calling any plays or anything like that. I'll be off in the stands just watching the scrimmage. Today, I'm nothing more than a football fan watching two teams have a little fun."

Clifton, Sean, and Daniel each take turns shaking the coach's hand then turn their attention to the St. Michael's players. They look menacing. At first glance, it is quite apparent that they are far bigger, but they also look like a polished, professional team with each member of the squad wearing the exact same outfit from top to bottom.

The Centerville players, in stark contrast, look like a bunch of ragtag kids that have gathered together to play football for fun at some random field. There is no connection between the players through colors or jersey, nor do they have matching equipment like St. Michael's does. Every member of the St. Michael's team is wearing matching cleats, the same colored gloves, same-colored wristbands, and same-colored socks. Not one thing looks out of order with any part of their overall appearances.

Jeremy can't help but be impressed. These guys clearly have their stuff together. He exhales loudly and faces Walter, who is standing there awe-struck by their competition. Next to Walter is Carlos. "Those are the guys that we are playing?" asks Carlos.

"Yup, that's the St. Michael's Falcons. They are one of the best teams in the state every single year," said Jeremy.

"They don't look that tough to me. Just because they know how to match their clothes doesn't mean they know how to play ball. Let's see if anyone over there can keep up with this," says Carlos. Carlos starts to stretch his legs and then jogs in place a bit to keep them warmed up.

The captains from both teams continue to talk in a circle. After a few minutes, they shake hands and part ways, walking back to their respective teams.

Clifton speaks, "Here are the rules. Fifteen minute quarters. If you score, you get six points. Period. That's the only scoring today. No points for stops, sacks, interceptions, or anything else. No kickoffs, either. The captains will call penalties if we see them, but don't expect there to be a lot of that. Quarterbacks will have five seconds to get rid of the ball; if no one's open after that time, it's a loss of a down. We are going to use a fifty-yard field and mark off ten-yard increments. Four downs to get ten yards, just like in a real game. No linemen this time,

178

except for the center. On offense there will be a center, QB, four receivers, and a running back. Defense, will have two linebackers, three corners, and two safeties. Each team is going to have ten minutes to quickly run through offense and defense before we start the game. Let's get going; we are going to get the ball first."

Jeremy and the rest of the offense begin to prepare. Jeremy stands in the middle, while his receivers line up on either side of him; Carlos is standing behind him. Sean calls a play from the line of scrimmage. Jeremy takes the ball and throws it to his first option. They run the play again; this time he tosses it to his second option on the play. They run play after play in this fashion until the time is up.

This is it. The offense huddles up around Daniel. "Listen up! Just relax out there and do what we've been practicing all week. Don't freak out because it's the St. Michael's Falcons; just run the plays the way I know you can run them." He calls a play and the offense jogs up to the line of scrimmage. Jeremy's heart is racing; how would he fare against a real top-tier high school defense?

The ball is hiked back to him, and someone on the sidelines begins to count, "One thousand one, one thousand two…" before he gets to three, the ball is out of Jeremy's hand and into Ricky's for a ten yard gain. Daniel calls another play, and the offense sets up. Jeremy takes receipt of the ball and glances over the defense. He pump fakes to his left, and then lets go of a perfect pass to Carlos. Carlos has blown past two defenders and reaches out to grab the spiraling ball. He catches it and surges into the endzone for a touchdown.

Centerville's sideline erupts in celebration. St. Michael's gets the ball and scores on their first play, going the distance of the field in a blur. After Centerville's opening-drive success, St. Michael's takes control of both sides of the ball. Jeremy and the offense are able to move the ball effectively, but they find it incredibly difficult to punch it into the endzone.

On defense, Centerville is simply no match for the powerful St. Michael's offense. They easily cruise up and down the field scoring at will. By halftime, the score is Centerville 12, St. Michael's 36.

Jeremy searches the faces of his teammates at halftime. They look dejected. Clifton tries, in vain, to rile up the troops, but it seems to have very little effect. Following the first half beat-down, the guys know that they can't compete with the level of talent St. Michael's has, no matter how hard they try.

The second half starts off about as bad as it can, with St. Michael's scoring on a three-play drive and then intercepting Jeremy's first throw. It has been less than two minutes into the third quarter, and Centerville is now down 48-12.

Jeremy doesn't, and will not, quit; but he does start to wonder if he is playing on the wrong team. Although he is happy to be playing with his friends, thoughts begin to creep back into his mind of what it would be like to play with the superior talent of St. Michael's. Their receivers are bigger and more explosive, their tight end is a complete beast, and they have two running backs that are just as fast, if not faster, than Carlos will ever be. The talent levels between the two teams are so lopsided that it almost doesn't seem fair that the two teams are playing on the same field.

At the end of the third quarter, Centerville's chances receive a little glimmer of hope. Jeremy hooks up with Ricky on a deep ball that goes for a touchdown making the score 48-24. Then, the defense forces a turnover. Jeremy, once again, finds Ricky deep in the end zone cutting the St. Michael's lead to three scores. Unfortunately, that's as close at Centerville is going to get. The final score is 60-36 in favor of St. Michael's.

At the end of the game, Coach Fletcher comes over to the Centerville side. "I just want to tell you boys that you put up one heck of a fight out there. It might not seem like it because of the score, but my team almost won a state title last year and is poised to go all the way this year. You scored six times on one of the best, if not the best, defenses in the state. That's saying something."

Coach motions for Jeremy to walk with him as he moves away from the rest of the team. "It's hard to try and do it all yourself, don't you think? You had a great game out there today, but that final result is going to keep happening to this team because they don't have enough quality players on either side of the ball. Look at it this way, if you were on our team as opposed to theirs, we would have won by fifty points without even breaking a sweat." The coach places a hand on Jeremy's shoulder but he is busily staring at the ground. "I'm not telling you this because I want you to be away from your friends; I'm telling you this because playing for me is the best choice for you. Look at today. That team's never going to win anything. They can't beat any of the good teams in the state, and you know it."

Jeremy doesn't want to admit it, but after today, he knows the coach is probably right. They scored on offense thanks largely to him and Ricky, both of whom may not be going to Centerville in the fall. Carlos has some serious skills, but he's new and doesn't know the offense yet. The rest of the team is, if Jeremy is going to be honest with himself, average at best, with a handful of exceptions.

"Jeremy, I've got to go and get on my bus, but I'll leave you with this. Would you rather be the guy that sticks by his teammates on the way to a losing season, and probably four straight losing seasons, or, do you want to be the guy that takes an already great team to repeated state titles? The choice is yours." The coach gives him a look and leaves to get onto the bus. The bus' engines roar to life, and they drive away leaving only a cloud of dust behind them.

"What did Coach want?" asks Ricky.

"Nothing much. He just wanted to talk to me about the game a little, that's all."

Walter walks in between Jeremy and Ricky. He put his arms around both of them. "Well, that sucked. How about we all head back to

182

my house, hop in the pool, order some food, and try to forget that this ever happened?"

Ricky responds, "I'm in."

Jeremy agrees, "Yeah, why not. I'm heading to California tomorrow with my dad, so it's my last time to hang out with you guys for a week."

"Well then, there must be a celebration!" exclaims Jeff from out of nowhere.

"Dude, where did you even come from?" asks Walter.

"I'm like a ninja. You can't hear me; sometimes you can't even see me, but I'm always there."

"You are so strange," says Ricky, "but, we love you anyway."

"Walter, go grab Zach, and let's head to your house" says Ricky. "I'm hot, I'm starving, and I could really use a jump in the pool."

The boys march to Walter's house through the excruciating heat. To this point, today has been the hottest day of the summer, with temperatures soaring close to 100. While they are walking, they talk very little about the beat down they just received. Instead, they focus more on what they can do better the next time they play. The conversation continues amongst the boys until they reach Walter's. Jeff elects to make yet another proclamation, "In honor of Jeremy's last night before he goes to California, I want to give him something to

183

remember me by." Jeff searches through the group until he sees Walter, "Walter, you have a bike, right?"

"Yeah, why?"

"You'll see in a minute."

Walter looks at Jeremy who just shrugs and says, "Like I ever know what that guy is doing."

Then Walter looks at Ricky.

"Don't look at me, I'm just as lost as the rest of you."

The boys get to the house and plop down heavily on chairs and couches in an attempt to regain some lost strength. Jeff does not. He walks right past all of them and out to the backyard. From inside, you can vaguely hear the shed door open in the backyard. This is followed abruptly by some loud banging sounds.

Jeremy turns to face Walter, "What the heck is he doing out there?"

"I have no idea, but whatever it is, I'm sure it's going to be entertaining."

Zach has been very quiet since the end of the game. He isn't used to getting beaten like that. Since there were no linemen playing in the game, there wasn't anything he could do about it either. This only made it that much worse for him. He finally breaks his silence, "Did you see the look on that coach's face in the stands? While they were tearing into us, he just sat there loving every second of it." Zach's facial expressions clearly demonstrate his disgust with the coach's actions. He drives a fist into the couch, "It makes me so mad that there was nothing I could do about it."

"Well, he is their coach, Zach; he should like to see his team do well," said Walter.

"It was more than that; it was almost as if he was trying to prove a point or something. I can't quite put my finger on it, but I really felt like he was trying to teach us a lesson. Like, hey, you guys can't play with the big boys in the state or something."

Jeremy sat there quietly listening to Zach. He didn't know why, but he knew that there is some truth to what Zach had said. When hearing that the two teams were going to be scrimmaging, he too felt that something was weird about the whole thing. During the game, he looked to the stands from time to time and could see exactly what Zach was talking about. It was as if the Coach was enjoying watching his team annihilate Centerville. More than that, it seemed arranged somehow, like the whole thing had been some big set-up or something. The more Jeremy thinks about it, the more certain he becomes of the coach's involvement. The coach did seem very confident when he was talking to Jeremy, almost arrogant. After all, his team had just clobbered Jeremy's in very convincing fashion. Could it be possible that the scrimmage was actually set up by Coach Fletcher and that he was trying to drive a point home to Jeremy specifically?

Moments later, Jeff's yelling from the backyard derails Jeremy's train of thought, "It is time for my next feat!" The boys all shoot up and run outside. Sitting next to the pool is a make-shift ramp comprised of rocks as a base and an old piece of plywood as a top. It is two feet away from the pool. Jeff is in perfect alignment with the ramp. His legs are holding him up and he has Walter's bike in between his legs. "It's that time again, friends! It's time for the Jeff show!"

Before anyone can say anything, Jeff speeds off. He pumps his legs as fast as he can as the bike climbs up the ramp with ease. He gets airborne and jumps free of the bike. He and the bike smash into the water and send up a huge wave racing out in all directions. He resurfaces to applause. "Thank you, thank you. Thank you all very much. You've been an incredible crowd!"

Jeff pushes the bike to the side of the pool where Zach effortlessly lifts it out of the water. "You're a maniac!" says Zach.

Jeff just smiles and kicks backwards, sending his body plunging into the cool water. The rest of the guys join him in the pool. The water, though warm from the heat of the day, feels soothing to them. Ricky jumps out of the pool and walks over to a plastic storage container. He pulls out a football and yells for Jeremy, "Hey, Savvy! Here, toss it to me while I jump in." Ricky throws the ball to Jeremy, who catches it and readies himself for the pass. Ricky sprints at full speed towards the water and hurdles himself through the air. Jeremy throws the ball in the perfect place. Ricky catches it just as his feet hit the water.

"You've just given me another idea!" says Jeff. "I'm going to ride the bike up the ramp, jump like I just did, but this time, Jeremy's going to toss the ball to me. I'm going to catch it as I land in the water. It's going to be one sweet-looking trick!"

Jeff hops out of the water and grabs the bike. He lines it up with the ramp, same as before, and looks at Jeremy. "Ok, this may take a try or two to get the timing down. I'm going to do exactly what I did last time. Once I'm free from the bike, hit me with it."

Jeremy nods as Jeff rockets off. Just as before, Jeff hits the ramp perfectly and launches his body and the bike towards the water. He puts his hands up indicating to Jeremy to toss the ball just as he releases his grip from the bike. The ball sails a little over his head and ricochets off the surface of the pool, sending water spraying into Walter's face. "Not cool, Jeremy!"

"Sorry, Walter."

Jeff resurfaces, "We didn't miss that by much. Let's give it another go." Jeff and the bike get out of the water with a little help from Zach. Jeff lines himself up for the third time and takes off towards the pool. He gets even more air this time as Jeremy releases the ball. Unlike the last one, this pass is perfect. It hits Jeff right in the hands, but he isn't able to secure the ball. The water forces the ball out of his grip as he sinks under the water.

His head pokes above the surface and Ricky shouts at him, "That's why you play defense! Nice catch, stone hands!"

All the guys laugh hysterically. For the next few hours, they play pool basketball and volleyball. Once that is finished, they all have a seat on the lounge chairs and relax.

"So, Jeremy," says Jeff. "What's this thing in California you're doing?"

"It's just this football camp that I'm going to."

Ricky throws the wet towel he used to dry off at Jeremy, "He's being modest as always. Savvy here has been invited to a very special camp at the Direct Athletics Facility in California." Hearing this, Zach jumps into the conversation, excitedly saying, "That's where all the great athletes train. You're probably going to see some of those guys up close while you are there. You're going to have to tell us all about it when you get back! Plus, I'll want to know all about the cool equipment they have. What exercises did you see guys doing, stuff like that."

"This guy, do you ever think of anything other than exercising?" asks Ricky.

"Yup! Girls, football, and video games. Those are my other three major areas of interest."

Walter changes the subject, "So Jeremy, have you decided where you're going to play next year? I'm sure today made the decision a little easier for you. Those guys are really good. If I were you, I may want to play there, too."

Zach grabs his wet towel off the ground and whips it at Walter. "Shut up, you! Jeremy can make up his own mind."

Jeremy shakes his head, "Believe it or not, I'm still not sure. Sure, they are good, but I think we've got some talent too. Also, I'd miss not playing on the same team as you bunch of crazy people."

With that, unprovoked, Jeff stands up from his chair and squeeze it tightly against his chest. He raises it a little off the ground so that he can move his feet and walks towards the pool. He reaches the edge, and jumps in, landing perfectly on the chair in the center of the pool. As he sinks, he looks over at Jeremy, "That's just one more thing to remember me by before your trip tomorrow!

16

Jeremy's father gives him a little shove, jostling one of his ear buds, which falls out. They have been in the air for four hours and still have over an hour to go. Jeremy's dad feels that now is a good time to begin the conversation he wanted to have with his son. He signals for Jeremy to remove the other ear bud. As Jeremy takes it out of his ear, his father asks, "So, have you thought any more about Centerville versus St. Michael's? I haven't gotten to talk to you about it since our last conversation."

Jeremy, still a little groggy from sleeping for the past two hours, tries to shake the cobwebs out of his head before answering. "Um, yeah. I've been thinking about it a lot actually. That butt-kicking we got courtesy of St. Michael's at the scrimmage kind of made me realize that no matter what we do, we aren't going to be as good as them, at least not any time soon."

"While that may be true, it's not the best attitude to have. Whenever I got beat playing at something, it made me want to get better, not quit. Plus, what about what you were saying before about not wanting to leave your friends? You know, friends are really important, especially in high school. As you know, I'm still good friends with some of my high school buddies to this day."

Jeremy is taken aback a bit by his father's words. "I know, and that's still a big deal to me. But, you and mom were making it sound like St. Michael's is the best place for my future. That's something that is hard to argue, and I'm not saying that I want to quit, I'm just saying that we got it handed to us by St. Michael's and that they are clearly better than us right now." Jeremy angrily shifts his body slightly onto his other side. "Besides, you guys were the ones saying that now's the time for me to be selfish and think about myself, right?"

"That's true, and we still want you to think about your future when you eventually make your decision. One thing we would also like you to consider is your importance to the actual town of Centerville. You know, they've never had an athlete of your caliber actually attend Centerville High. You could be the best player in any sport to graduate from Centerville, ever. That's pretty cool, don't you think?"

Jeremy is completely confused at this point, "What's happening here? I don't get it. You and mom were making it sound like this was such an easy decision for me. Now, you're all about me going to Centerville. What's the deal?"

His father moves uncomfortably, "There's no deal here. We just want to make sure that you understand that you are a special type of kid. Whether you know it or not, there are people in this town that look up to you. All the young guys idolize you for winning a championship. I just don't know if that's something that you're going to get at St. Michael's."

Jeremy goes to say something else but stops. He throws his hands in the air in frustration and puts the ear buds back into his ears.

191

After the exchange, the two sit in silence for the remainder of the trip. Jeremy feels even more perplexed now than ever before. Why was his father pulling a complete 180 on him now?

About an hour later, Jeremy hears the familiar ding inside the airplane. He looks over at this father who is still reading his magazine. David stretches, puts the magazine away, and tosses a piece of gum into his mouth as the airplane makes its descent.

"Want a piece?"

Jeremy nods and accepts the gum from his dad.

Once the plane lands safely and the signal is given, David stands up from his seat and opens the storage compartment above his head. He reaches in, grabs his son's backpack, and hands it to him. He fishes around in the compartment a little more, finds his leather attaché case and takes it out. He checks a few things in one of the side compartments of the bag and shoulders it. "Once we get off the plane, I'll call your mom to let her know we got here safe."

"Already texted her, Dad."

"Wow, that was fast. Ok, great. One less thing for me to do."

The two wait for the line in front of them to move and eventually enter the procession to get off the plane. Jeremy is excited. He knows that there is more to discuss between him and his father, but that can be put aside for now. He has never been to California before. More than that, he is eager to be going to what is arguably the best football camp for incoming high school freshman in the country.

They exit the plane and head down the ramp in search of the location of the Baggage Claim area. As they come off the ramp, there is a large board in front of them listing all of the flight details and Baggage Claim area information. David scans the list of names and numbers, "Looks like we are at number 7. Let's hop to it; got a big day ahead of us."

The camp is set to start tomorrow, so David wants to try and get some touristy things in today for his son. He and his wife have been to California a number of times in the past, so he knows a few places he feels Jeremy will really enjoy that aren't too far away. The two wait at the conveyor belt as dozens and dozens of pieces of luggage rattle around, moving in a serpentine-style pattern. David locates their bags and rips them off the luggage carousel. Then, the two head towards the car rental area. "Hey Dad, can we rent something really cool? I mean, it's pretty nice out, and we could get a convertible…or maybe a sports car, or a convertible sports car!"

"Sure we can; you're paying, right?"

"I don't have any money."

"Then I think we are just going to stick to the one your mother picked out for us. Trust me, I'd like to rent something really nice too, but this flight wasn't cheap." Jeremy's head sinks a bit as he nods. Feeling a little disappointed, he continues to follow his father to the rental car desk.

"Hello, I'd like to pick up my reservation; it's under David Savage." The clerk behind the counter smiles brightly and begins to punch a few keys on the keyboard. "Let's see what we have here, Savage, Savage, Savage…here we are. It looks like you have our standard class car. You have a selection from either a Ford Focus or a Toyota Corolla." Jeremy rolls his eyes, "Not exactly exciting options, Dad." The woman behind the desk overhears Jeremy. She punches the keys a few more times, "You know what, it looks like we had a late cancellation on a certain car I think you two will like very much. How about I upgrade you, no extra charge of course, and you two have some fun here in California?"

"Cool. What is it?" Jeremy blurts out.

"How about a Ford Mustang convertible?"

"Wow, that's very nice of you to do that for us. I really appreciate it. Are you sure this won't cause you any trouble?" asks David.

"No troubles at all. Let's just update your paperwork and get you two on the road." The woman makes a few quick keystrokes. Suddenly, a printer behind her springs to life. "Here we are." She points to the paper while talking to David. "Here's your price, same as before, but here's the new vehicle information."

David takes a pen off the countertop and scribbles his name. Jeremy peeks over his dad's shoulder so he can see the woman's face, "Thanks a lot!" says Jeremy.

194

David puts an arm around his son, "Thanks again. This is really great. Something tells me that we are going to like this car a little better than what we would have."

"No problem, just remember us the next time you need to rent a car."

"Absolutely!"

With that, David extends the handle of his rolling suitcase, gives it a quick tilt to set it on its wheels, and walks away from the counter. They pass through a pair of floor-to-ceiling sliding glass doors and out into the parking lot. The excitement in Jeremy's voice makes it sound like he is practically yelling, "Which one do you think it is?"

David looks down at the keys in his hand and thumbs the unlock and lock button a few times. A loud, 'beep, beep,' sound can be heard directly to the right of where they are standing. The large duffel bag that Jeremy is using as a suitcase is getting heavier the farther he walks. It is starting to weigh down his shoulder, but he doesn't care. He turns to his right and starts to walk quickly in the direction of the sound. "Hit it again, Dad!" Jeremy calls out. This time, David thumbs the button a few more times.

"Found it! It's over here." David catches up to his son. Jeremy's duffel bag and carry on backpack are on the ground beside him. As David takes his place next to his son, Jeremy is simply staring at the sight before him. David whistles loudly, "Not bad, huh?"

195

After football, Jeremy's next great love is cars. Ever since his first Matchbox car, he has been hooked. "I'm so happy that woman upgraded us to this, Dad; check this thing out!"

David can't hide his own enthusiasm. Besides, it's not like Jeremy is the only one in the house that enjoys a sports car. David stands his suitcase and pushes the handle down. He circles around the car taking it all in. He runs a finger along the beautiful paint job as he continues his circle around the vehicle.

David recognizes right away, that this car is the brand new model. The black paint job is so clean and new that he can see his reflection in it perfectly. The top is already down, simply waiting to be driven by him. David pops open the trunk using the controller on the key ring. He gently places his bag inside. "Hey, Jeremy, are we going to drive it, or are you just going to keep staring at it?"

Jeremy smirks and places his duffel bag and carry-on in the trunk next to his father's suitcase. He picks up his backpack and tosses that in the trunk also, which is actually much roomier than Jeremy thought it would be. He admires the car a little longer on his way to the passenger side door. He gently opens the door and slides into the supple leather seat. He removes a pair of sunglasses from his pocket and places them on his face.

"Where to, Dad?"

David takes his attaché case and places it in the back seat. He hops into the driver's seat and takes out his own sunglasses, Maui

196

Jim's. They were a bit of a splurge for him, but he didn't care; he loves those sunglasses. They completely block out the sun, and he has owned them for over ten years now, which he feels is a pretty good return for his money. He puts the sunglasses on and glances at his son, "I've got a few things in mind that I think you'll like."

With that, he puts the keys in the ignition and starts the engine. It booms to life instantly; the exhaust growls loudly. David pushes down the gas pedal a few times and smiles to himself as he listens to the engine's loud response. The two buckle their seatbelts and explode out of the parking lot into the welcoming sunshine.

17

The next day, Jeremy and his dad arrive at the training facility an hour early to see if they can get a quick tour before the camp begins. David slowly cruises through the parking lot, scouring it for a good spot to park. He finally settles on one. He slowly pulls the car into the spot. He lets the car idle for another second then cuts off the engine. Jeremy reaches into the backseat and takes hold of his backpack, which is stuffed full of extra clothes and his favorite pair of cleats. He shoulders the bag and scans the outside of the building.

It is one of the biggest structures he has ever seen. The front is all glass, which reflects the brightly shining California sun. The words 'Direct Athletics Performance' are etched in huge letters high above the doorway. All along the front of the building are beautifully landscaped flowers, trees, and bushes, which remind Jeremy of resorts he's seen in commercials. David opens the trunk and grabs hold of Jeremy's large duffel bag. He lifts it out of the trunk and holds it in his hand while looking at his son. He smirks, "Hey, Jeremy, think Mom would like it if we made the front of the house look like that?"

Jeremy laughs and just shakes his head. "Yeah, right, Dad. Can you imagine how much time it must take to do that?"

They approach the front doors, which are just as impressive as the rest of the building. The doors are also made out of glass, with bright silver metal wrapped around the outside of the glass acting like a frame. The Direct Athletics Performance name is also etched into the two doors directly in the center. The handles are thick, and as Jeremy attempts to pull one of the doors open, he quickly realizes just how heavy they are. He struggles a bit to get the door open with just one hand. His dad muses, "Jeez, even opening the door is a workout here."

"Ha ha, very funny, Dad." Jeremy finally fights the door open and walks through the opening. He instantly feels a waft of chilled air hit his warm body. A little shiver ripples over his skin as he adjusts to the new temperature. Right in front of them stands a desk made out of the same metal that frames the front doors. Once again, the Direct Athletics Performance logo can be seen sitting in the center of the desk front. This time the logo is in big, bold, black block letters. There are three television screens on the wall behind the desk, each tuned into a different sports station. On the screens are images depicting the highlights from the night before.

A few feet from either side of the desk are two large spiraling staircases that lead up to a second floor. Behind the desk, sits a very attractive young woman. Jeremy guesses that she is probably in her early twenties. She has flawless skin and a youthful-looking face. She is wearing a tight-fitting, black polo shirt with the Direct Athletics Performance name emblazoned in bright red letters on the top right corner. She also has on a name tag that reads, "Ashley" on the left-hand side of the shirt. Her skin is a beautifully tanned light brown, and her dark brown hair is pulled back tightly in a ponytail. Although she is currently sitting, it is easy to see that she is in fantastic shape. Jeremy's dad sends a light elbow into his son's side and whispers to him, "Stop drooling, Buddy."

"Hello. Welcome to Direct Athletics Performance. How may I help you today?"

"Hello. My son is one of the invitees to the camp this week. We are hoping to take a tour of the facility before the start of camp."

Ashley smiles, "Sure thing. Do you have all of his paperwork completed?"

David unfolds a few papers that had been stashed in his pocket. He extends them to her, "Here you go."

She takes the papers from his hand and moves her eyes to the computer screen. "All righty, let me just double-check everything here and make sure that he's in the system." She raps on the keys for a little while, and then looks up. "Great! Looks like you guys are all set. If you give me a few minutes, I'll get one of our trainers to give you a tour. You won't have too much time, though, because sign-ins actually start in a little over a half hour. For now you can have a seat in the waiting area while I get someone for you." She hands the paperwork back to David, "Your son is going to need these when he gets officially checked in at the beginning of camp." David takes the papers from her and hands them to Jeremy, "Here, hang on to these, and don't lose them." Jeremy takes the papers and crams them into his already stuffed backpack.

A few moments later, a short, but very stout, man enters the waiting area. He has a massive chest and bulging biceps, which look even bigger in his extremely tight T-shirt that appears to be too small for him. He extends a massive hand towards David. "Hello. My name is Eric. I'm one of the trainers here. I'll be the one showing you guys around." His voice is powerful and, Jeremy thought, a little intimidating.

David grips the man's hand and shakes it vigorously, "Sounds great. My name is David Savage, and this is my son, Jeremy."

Eric stretches his hand out towards Jeremy, "Pleased to meet you, Jeremy."

Jeremy takes hold of the man's hand and shakes it.

"Wow, you've got quite a grip on you kid, just like your dad here. Let me guess, quarterbacks?"

Jeremy nods his head up and down indicating that the man's guess had been correct.

"I knew it. Every good quarterback that comes here has a wicked grip. So, Ashley informs me that you guys want to take a look at the facility. Is there anything in particular you want to see? Before you respond, just so you both know, all of the participants of the camp are going to get a full tour right after registration. This place is pretty big, and it takes a little while to get around all of it, so we won't be able to get in everything before you need to get going."

Jeremy looks to his father, "Well, is there anything in particular you want to see?"

David thinks for a moment and looks at Eric, "You're the expert. I am just hoping to get to see some of the amenities that you have here. I've heard everything is state-of-the-art and really first class all the way."

Eric smiles, "Follow me. I've got a few things in mind that I think you'll like."

The three pass by the desk where Ashley is still sitting and hike up one of the staircases. They come to a landing with long hallways stretching in front of them as well as to the right and the left. Eric turns his head just a bit and says over his shoulder, "Follow me." They take a left hand turn and head down one of the hallways. After about twenty feet, the wall on the right changes from typical painted sheetrock to all glass. Eric stops and faces the glass, "Check this out; this is our Aquatics Center."

David and Jeremy step close to the wall of glass and look out. David breathes out a barely audible, "Wow."

Below them is a massive, wide-open room. There are three Olympic-sized pools, four smaller pools, and five extremely large hot tubs. Jeremy asks, "What are the smaller pools for?"

"We use those for guys that need to either rehab in the water or want to train in a smaller environment."

Jeremy asks, "Why are there so many hot tubs?"

202

"Believe it or not, those aren't all hot tubs. Three of them are your traditional style hot tub; the other two are actually cold tubs. We have more of both kinds of tubs in the men's and women's locker rooms as well. I figure you guys might get a kick out of this. If you take a look at the far end of the first pool, you should see someone that I think you'll both recognize."

David and Jeremy are captivated by the sheer enormity of the room. They have hardly even noticed that there are actually people in there as well. Jeremy searches in the direction Eric has indicated and immediately knows who the individual is. His eyes grow wide, and he looks to his father, who is standing with his mouth hanging open, gaping at the sight. "Is that who I think it is?"

His father doesn't say a word; he just keeps staring in disbelief. Eric smiles, "Yes sir, that right there is Brady Clark, football's league champ and MVP last year. He trains here all spring and summer to get ready for the season. Some say he's the best quarterback to ever play. Believe it or not, he's actually a really cool guy once you get to know him."

"You mean you've actually talked to him?" inquires Jeremy.

"Talked to him? Heck, I train him most of the time. That is, when he is doing strength-training work outs. That's my specialty; I don't do any of the cardio, stretching, Pilates, or any of that other kind of stuff. Come on. There's more I want to show you guys."

They continue past the aquatics center and descend some stairs. "Here, the focus is solely on the athlete, so we try to make sure we have every possible thing they could want or dream of" says Eric. He continues talking as they round a corner, "But, you have to remember, these guys are used to having the very best of everything. Every big time Division I college program has amenities that would make your head spin, and the professionals just take that to a whole other level. So, here, we have to go even one above that." They come to a large set of double doors. Eric pushes past the doors and holds one open for David and Jeremy to pass through.

"Check this out" say Eric. David and Jeremy stand in disbelief as they look around the room. Jeremy guesses it is a combination locker room and lounge room area. It is the best appointed room he has ever seen in his life and that includes any room in Walter's house. As they stand at the threshold and peer in, Jeremy takes extra care to fully absorb the conveniences contained within the room. Before him are large lockers which cover the wall on the left side of the room. The floor is covered with a thick, plush wall-to-wall carpet. The letters D and A are inscribed within a circle and the Direct Athletics logo is embroidered perfectly in the carpet below the letters. In front of each locker are individual benches with leather tops on them, offering comfortable seating while the member changes.

On the right, there are large windows which overlook a seating area and game room. In that area, Jeremy can discern that there are three rows of high-end recliners, which are placed before an entire wall of flat screen televisions. From his vantage point, Jeremy can also see that every game console that exists is on the AV stand to the right of the wall. On the base of the cabinet, are controllers to the systems which are strewn all over the place. Next to the sitting area are three pool tables, two air hockey tables, a ping pong table, and actual arcade games. Flat screen televisions line the walls around the tables, as well.

As the three slowly continue into the room, Jeremy notices that there is a wall separating the lounge area from the food area, which is perhaps the most impressive of all the things Jeremy has seen to this point. On a large table are four different types of cereals in plastic containers with a spout at the bottom to disburse the contents. There are three refrigerators, each housing various types of meats and all sorts of odd foods. There are five blenders, every kind of protein an athlete could want, and fruits that Jeremy has never even seen before. There is an entire cabinet of vitamins, supplements, and minerals. There is a fountain beverage area much like one that you would see in a fast food chain or restaurant that dispenses juices and different flavored water, as well as energy drinks. There are vending machines which contain varying types of potato chips, candy bars, gummy snacks, energy bars, and everything else in between. It is the most food Jeremy has ever seen in one room.

Eric comes up behind them, "Pretty insane, huh?"

"It is," says David, "I can't believe there's so much junk food here."

"Well, you have to remember, some of these athletes can burn thousands of calories per workout. Although the vast majority of them watch what they eat diligently, when you're burning those kinds of calories, a snack every now and then isn't going to do any harm."

Jeremy doesn't even hear the conversation his father and Eric are having about the food.. Instead, he just continues to take in all the sights around him. David stands in the center of the room completely awe-struck. He puts a hand on Jeremy's shoulder and leans in close to his son's ear, "One day, you're going to be a member here."

Eric checks his watch, "I think we are going to have to cut this tour a little short; sign-ups begin shortly and we really should get Jeremy back."

Eric guides them back to the waiting area. He turns to face Jeremy and smiles, "Figured I'd give you one more look at Ashley before we head out to sign-ups."

The three continue on through two more sets of doors and eventually arrive in a very large room. The room resembles a lecture hall found at most colleges. At the front of the hall is a collection of large tables. Each table has two men sitting behind it with clipboards. On the tables facing out are tented pieces of paper with letters on them. Jeremy scans them from left to right. The papers read: A-D, E-H, I-L, M-P, Q-T, U-Z.

Eric points a finger at the paper marked Q-T, "Jeremy, that's where you need to go to check in. One of the guys behind the table will formally check you in and give you a bag filled with stuff from Direct Athletics. Then he'll tell you where your apartment is and who your roommate will be."

"Apartment?" asks David.

Eric chuckles, "Yeah, that's just what we call them. Basically, they are like really high end dorm rooms. We had them built five years ago for events such as this or when whole teams come here to train."

David nods in understanding, "That's pretty cool. What's in the bag?"

"Just a bunch of stuff like T-shirts, water bottles, stickers, socks, shorts. Basically, anything we can put our logo on is in that bag. Well, my work here is done. Mr. Savage, this area is restricted for players only so, if you wouldn't mind following me back out, I'd appreciate it. The practice fields in the back are open to relatives. If you'd like to see some of what Jeremy's going to be doing here, I can bring you out there. Jeremy and the other boys will be out in an hour or so, depending on how long this part takes."

"Yeah, that would be great" says David. He faces Jeremy, "You have all your paperwork, right?"

"Yeah, Dad. I got it all."

"Ok, well, I guess I'll see you outside at some point. Listen, Jer, have fun and learn everything you can from these people. They are the best."

David turns and follows Eric out of the hall. Jeremy shuffles over to the table Eric had pointed out. One of the men looked him squarely in the face, "Name?"

"Jeremy Savage."

The man takes his pen and searches the names on the list. He arrives at Jeremy's name and gives it a quick check. He reaches behind him and grabs a soft bag with the Direct Athletics logo on it. "Here is your welcome gift. You're all set. Your roommate for the week is going to be Jackson Jones. Have a seat wherever you like. The coaches will arrive shortly."

Jeremy takes the bag and finds an open seat. The hall is beginning to fill in with kids. Noise reverberates loudly off the walls as the hall continues to fill-in. Jeremy sits, looking out at the soon-to-be high schoolers. He wonders to himself if any of them are having the same problems he is having. Would any of them have trouble leaving friends behind to play at a better school? He isn't sure of the answer, but he is sure of one thing: he wants this to be his life more than anything else in the world.

18

Jeremy has learned a lot in the first few days of camp. The trainers have shown him new ways to increase strength in his shoulder as well as how to build core stability through a number of different exercises; all of which Zach is going to love to try out. The coaches have instructed him on his footwork and how to progress through reads even faster than he already could. Jeremy is completely enthralled with everything that he is learning. He is like a sponge, and all of the coaches and trainers are incredibly impressed with his work ethic and abilities. Typically, kids going into high school think that they already know everything there is to know. Due to this, some of the athletes prove to be a challenge to coach. This often results in limited growth, despite tremendous physical gifts. Jeremy is not like that at all. He possesses all of the physical gifts that coaches dream of, but he is arguably the most coachable player most of them have ever come into contact with, making him a camp favorite.

During the week Jeremy also learns that out of the seven quarterbacks at the camp, five of them are either going to private or prep schools. The lone quarterback going to a public high school happens to be his roommate, Jackson Jones.

Jackson is from Florida and gets to play football whenever he wants, thanks to Florida's year-round sunshine. Jackson is a dual-sport athlete excelling in both football and track. Apparently, Jeremy learns,

209

Jackson is not only arguably the best young quarterback from his state, he is also one of the fastest on the track. On the field, he is an absolute nightmare. He can not only pass, he can run with superior speed, as well. Jeremy also finds out while participating in a certain drill, that Jackson can catch nearly anything thrown at him too. Despite the fact that he and Jackson have completely different quarterbacking styles, the two become fast friends while rooming together.

Although Jeremy has some speed, he is more of the prototypical pocket passer than anything else. He stands tall in the pocket and has an absolute howitzer for an arm. Jackson is a threat to run any time he touches the ball, but he can also sling it around if he needs to as well. The two learn a lot from each other, due to their opposing quarterbacking styles.

One day after practice finishes, Jeremy finds Jackson and talks to him, trying to figure out why he has decided to go to a public school rather than a private school. "Hey, Jackson, mind if I ask you a question?"

Jackson finishes untying his cleats and pulls them off. He tosses them into his bag and takes out his sneakers, "No, what's up, Savvy?" He puts his sneakers on and stretches out a bit before jumping up to his feet. "By the way," said Jackson, "you were pretty nasty out there today throwing that ball. I'm not saying you're as good as me or anything, but you've got some skills."

"Thanks."

Jackson slings the bag containing his cleats over his shoulder and begins to walk.

"Walk with me, Savvy; let me hear what's on your mind."

"I am wondering why a guy like you is going to a public school and not some prestigious private school to play football. I mean, you're definitely good enough to play wherever you want."

Jackson laughs, "Thanks for the compliment, and, yes, I am that good, but a private school? That's not my style, you know. I want to be able to freestyle when I'm on the field. I've had a few coaches approach me about playing, but they want me to fit into *their* system rather than working their system around me. I met with the public school coach, and he thinks that I'm good enough to build an offense around; he gets me. So, that's where I'm going to go play. Come to think of it, I haven't heard you say where you're going yet, how about you? You going to be a preppy boy at some hoity-toity prep school where you've got to wear a uniform every day or what?"

"To tell you the truth, I haven't made up my mind yet. I really need to, though. The Monday I get back from this camp, double-sessions are going to start. I have to know where I'm going to go by then."

Jackson hikes up his bag, "Don't let anybody rush you, Savvy; you do your thing. You're a superstar, just like me. Look at where we are! Kids our age would kill to be here right now. Coaches fall all over themselves for talent like us. So, stop stressing, and just let it come to you."

"So, you think the decision is just going to all-of-a-sudden come to me?"

"Yup, it's going to be like divine intervention or something. I'm telling you; when the time comes, you'll just know what to do. All you've got to do is trust yourself."

The two walk off the field and into the main facility to grab some food, continuing their conversation as they go.

On the third day of camp, one of the coaches makes it a personal point to find David, who is watching everything from the sidelines with zeal. The coach finds David and starts a conversation with him, "Your son is really going to go places. I just have to tell you how fascinated I am by him. He's the most talented pure passer out here by a mile, but he isn't cocky and has no problem taking criticisms. He truly is one of a kind."

David loves every second of this interaction. "Yeah, he's just always been that way. He's always been the one that stays after practice to do extra work, regardless of the fact that he's the best on the team. He never gets angry, and he never talks back. He takes what anyone tells him to heart and really tries to improve his game based off suggestions. Unfortunately, my wife and I can't take any of the credit away from him, although we'd like to! He's so passionate about football; he really loves the game to his core."

The coach sticks around talking with David for a little while longer before rejoining the group. The more Jeremy plays, the more it becomes apparent to David just how good of a player his son truly is. Every quarterback at the camp is ridiculously talented; each having the ability to throw daggers while also demonstrating near pin-point accuracy. David knows that Jeremy can throw, and he knows that no one in Centerville can touch his skills. But, being at this camp, he now sees that no one in the country can hold a candle to Jeremy as a complete package.

Day four simply emphasizes what David is already beginning to believe; Jeremy really is the best of the best. Day four at the camp is what they call, 'Stat's Day.' 'Stat's Day' is modeled after The Combine. The Combine is where hopeful collegiate athletes compete in a series of challenges and tasks in preparation for the draft.

The participants of this camp run 40-yard dashes to assess speed and shuttle drills to test agility. Then, the different positions break off into their own groups to run through a predetermined set of challenges, which will be tabulated into a score. Jeremy and the quarterbacks are going to compete in a series of trials testing accuracy, arm strength, agility, and decision making.

First up is the 40-yard dash. The quarterbacks gather together. One by one, they each run as fast as they can for forty yards. There is a coach at the end marker telling them their times as they finish. Jeremy runs a 5.0, which he thinks is pretty descent.

The guys come together and walk to the next challenge. Jackson searches out and finds Jeremy, "Savvy, what was your time?"

"Pretty good, 5.0. It's the first time I've ever been clocked running a forty."

Jackson looks stunned, "That was the first time you've been timed? What? I've been getting timed since I was like eight."

"Yeah, you run track! So, what did you run?"

Jackson grins smugly, "You don't want to know. It's just going to make you feel bad about yourself, and I don't know if I can be responsible for that."

"Very funny. Don't worry, I know you're faster than me. What did you get?"

"4.5"

"Damn! 4.5? That's fast! Maybe you were right; I do feel bad now."

The two laugh as the group arrives at the cone drills, which are designed to test their agility. Once again, Jackson dominates while Jeremy comes in a respectable third place.

After the first two challenges, the next two are dominated by Jeremy. The third task tests arm strength. The guys are to throw the ball as far as they can. To know exactly how far someone throws, the field is marked, and the footballs have one nose of the ball dipped in paint. This way, when it lands the paint spot will show how far the ball has traveled. The first three guys all get the ball just across the forty yard

214

line. Jackson heaves one a little over forty-five yards, with which he appears to be very happy as he struts back to the group. Jeremy, however, uncorks one that soars over fifty yards in the air, besting everyone by at least five yards.

Next up is decision making. In this challenge, there are flat targets set about on the field. Some of the targets have bulls-eyes on them, the others are painted red. Once the challenge starts, the coach manipulates the targets with some sort of remote control. The remote control pops the targets up and sets it back down. If a target comes up with a bulls-eye on it, you are to throw at it. If a red one comes up, you aren't supposed to throw. If you hit a bulls-eye target, you get points; if you throw at a red target, you lose points. If you hit a red target, you lose even more points.

The challenge seems very simple, except that the coach is moving the targets up and down very quickly, forcing the quarterbacks to make snap decisions. Jeremy totals a score of 125 points; the next highest is 105.

The final challenge is the one everybody has been waiting for: the accuracy challenge. This time, the targets are set up on either sideline of the field. Using a remote control similar to the last challenge, the coach will press a button and send the targets moving from left to right. The quarterbacks throw ten balls at the moving targets to acquire points. Once again, the tips of the balls are painted to show exactly where the targets have been hit. The targets are set up like bulls-eyes.

215

The outer ring is blue, then yellow, and the smallest ring is red. If you hit the blue, it is twenty-five points. Yellow is fifty, and red is one hundred. As the quarterbacks begin to warm-up, one of the coaches steps forward. "There is a twist to this event. A twist that I think you will all like. It may put a little more pressure on you all, but, hey, this is football. This challenge will be monitored and viewed by a special guest: none other than Mr. Brady Clark."

Everyone stands there in silence as Brady Clark walks over to the testing area. Here he is, the reigning MVP, the best quarterback on the planet. He is here to watch a group of kids throw around a football. He casually strides up to the coaches and shakes their hands one-by-one. He then turns to face the group of seven prodigies. "I, too, was an invitee to this same camp. To tell you the truth, it doesn't seem like it was all that long ago that I was standing exactly where you all are right now. As a matter of fact, I believe that I still hold the camp record for this event with a score of 625 points." He checks the coaches who are nodding their heads, confirming that he is indeed correct and is still the record holder. "I'm excited to see what today's best can do. I want you all to bring your best to this event; you're going to need it. Good luck, gentlemen."

He joins the coaches on the sideline. Due to Jeremy's overall point lead, he is slated to go last, with Jackson right before him. The first three guys have real difficulty with the challenge, possibly because the best quarterback in the universe is watching them. None of them are able to amass more than two hundred points. Two of them even miss six of the targets completely. The next guy up is much better. He hits half of the targets for a total of two hundred and fifty points. This positive trend continues with the next participant, as well; he is able to hit one bull's eye, three yellows and two blues for a total of three hundred points.

The last two up are Jackson and Jeremy. Jackson takes a deep breath and exhales, "I don't know, Savvy. After watching the first bunch of guys go, maybe this challenge is tougher than I think it is."

"Just relax and throw; it's not life or death out there," says Jeremy.

"I like you, Savvy. I hope you always keep that coolness about you. Well, here I go." Jackson's turn starts off rocky, as he misses the first three targets. On the next two, he hits yellows, giving him one hundred points. This is followed by a miss and then a bull's-eye which gives him two hundred points with three throws left. On the next target, the ball slips a little out of Jackson's hand as he completes his throwing motion. The ball just nicks the blue for twenty-five more points. The next throw is an absolute strike, smashing nearly dead center. One throw left and three hundred-twenty five points earned so far. He is already the leader and looking to add a bit more on the final throw. The target moves, and he lets the ball go. It strikes just inside the yellow area for an additional fifty points. This gives him a grand total of three hundred and seventy-five points.

"Try to top that, Savvy!" says Jackson.

Before he begins his turn, Jeremy analyzes the targets, trying to get an exact read on their distances. The coach tells him to get ready, and Jeremy reaches for the first ball. His first throw is a bull's-eye. He grabs for the second, another bulls-eye. The third and fourth also hit the target, nearly bull's-eyes themselves, but just miss the center and strike the yellow parts of the targets for fifty points each. The next two throws are the best throws he has ever made in his life, nailing the targets right in the center. Six throws down, five hundred points already for Jeremy.

The next throw sails on him, missing the target. The eighth throw gets him right back on target, crashing into the red area once again, for yet another bull's-eye. 600 points and two throws left. The ninth ball is elevated a little, but is still accurate enough to hit the blue area of the target, giving him another twenty-five points. This ties Jeremy for the camp record with 625 points. One more hit will give him the best score ever and send Brady Clark into second place.

The final throw is by far the most difficult to make. The target is forty yards away and is the fastest moving. Jeremy hardens his nerves and reaches for the final ball. He sets his feet and watches as the target moves swiftly from left to right. He quickly calculates the distance of the target along with its speed and initiates his faultless throwing motion. The football blasts out of his hand, carving its way through the air towards the mobile target. The throw has so much force, it actually knocks the target off of its track and onto its back. The group makes

218

their way to the target, anxious to see where Jeremy has hit it. There, a deep orange spot could be seen inside the smallest ring of red for yet another bull's eye.

The other six players go wild and raise Jeremy up on their shoulders. He has done it. He has beaten the greatest quarterback to ever play the game in an accuracy competition. Not only has he beaten him, he does so by a hundred points, for a final total of 725!

After the celebration concludes, the coaches blow the whistle to indicate the end of the day's events. Jeremy is looking through the faces on the sideline, searching for his father when he feels a tap on his shoulder. He turns around to see Brady Clark standing before him. "Not bad, kid. What's your name?"

Jeremy's body goes rigid; he feels like he is paralyzed. "It's uh…my name is…Jeremy."

"Jeremy, I'm Brady Clark. It's nice to formally meet the kid that took my crown from me."

Jeremy just stands there, immobilized by the complete and utter shock of speaking in person to his idol. He opens his mouth, "Sorry about that. I didn't mean to score more points than you."

Brady laughs and pats Jeremy on the back, "It's ok, and of course you wanted to score more than me. That's what drives athletes like us. We want to be the best. If I were in your shoes, I would have wanted to have the best score too."

As the two converse, Jeremy's dad finds his way over to them. "Mr. Clark, this is my dad, David Savage."

"Nice to meet you, Mr. Savage. I'm not sure if you know this already, but your son just took my title from me for best score in the accuracy competition."

David, like his son, is a little shell-shocked. It has only been a few months since he and Jeremy had been watching as Brady Clark threw touchdown after touchdown on his way to a league championship and MVP award. "It's so nice to meet you, Mr. Clark. I've got to say, my son and I are huge fans of yours. This is a real treat for us."

Brady puts his hands on his hips, "I've got a great idea. What are you two doing tonight for dinner?"

David replies, "We don't really have any plans yet, why?"

"Fantastic! Then, you two are going to come to my place tonight for dinner. I'm not taking no for an answer."

Brady takes his phone out of his pocket, "David, what's your number? I'll text you my address."

David sneaks a glance at his son, trying to restrain the smile that is fighting to burst its way to the surface. He gives Brady the number. David's phone vibrates; he looks at the screen which depicts a short message that lists the address for tonight.

"Jeremy, why don't you give me your number too? This way, I can keep in touch with you throughout the season. If you have any questions at all, feel free to text or call me anytime. I remember what it was like to be in your shoes. High school can be tough; colleges are going to try and contact you day and night, begging you to choose their school. Take it from someone who's been there, it helps to have someone to talk to that doesn't stand to gain anything from your decisions."

Jeremy can't believe that Brady Clark is offering to not only have him and his father over for dinner, but also to mentor him.

"I look forward to seeing you guys tonight. You both like steak?"

Jeremy and David both nod. "Yeah, definitely" says David.

"That sounds awesome," says Jeremy.

"Great! Then I'll see you both tonight. Let's say, seven o'clock?"

"Works for us," says David.

With that, Brady turns around and walks back towards the training center.

Jeremy can't believe the day he is having. He has won the overall 'Stat's Day' competition for quarterbacks, he beat his hero's best score, which just so happens to be the best score in the history of the camp, and now, he and his father are going to dine with the best football player on the planet. He wonders how this day could get any better.

19

David's cell phone vibrates in his pocket. He takes it out and looks at the screen; it is his wife, Jessica. He swipes a finger across the screen and puts the phone to his ear, "Jess, you're not going to believe this! Jeremy was incredible today; he even broke a record!"

On the other end of the phone, Jessica is trying to do her best to listen to her excited husband while waiting to for an opportunity to break the bad news to him.

"Jess, you should have seen him out there; you would have been so proud! He was the best in his group and set the all-time accuracy record at the camp!"

"Wow, that's amazing. Is he with you now?"

"No, he went inside to shower up because they are done for the day. But listen to this; we got to meet Brady Clark. He's here training for the season."

Jessica may not watch a lot of football, especially when compared to her husband and son, but she knows exactly who Brady Clark is. The quarterback is everywhere. Billboards, commercials, you can't go an entire day without seeing his face somewhere.

"That's pretty exciting. Jeremy must be beside himself."

"Not only did we get to meet him, he invited us over to his place for dinner tonight! You should have seen Jeremy's face when he asked us. Apparently, he has soft spot for young quarterbacks, probably because Jeremy reminds him of himself when he was younger or something."

All of this is just making what she is about to say all the more difficult, "Jeremy must be loving life right now."

"Yeah, him and me both!"

Jessica fights back the tears in her voice, "David, I have to tell you something. It's not good. I'm not sure you are going to want to tell Jeremy right away, especially since you're going to be eating with his favorite player tonight. It's just going to make him upset."

The smile falls from David's face, and his heart begins to race in his chest, "Are you ok?"

"I'm fine, it's not me. It's Ricky's dad; it's Doug."

David has been dreading a phone call like this for a long while. He has tried, numerous times, to tell Doug that he can't treat his body the way he does, day-in and day-out, and not expect something bad to happen. "What happened? Is he all right?"

Jessica struggles with how to begin, "No, he isn't ok."

"What happened? How bad is it?"

"He's gone, David." The tears burst from her eyes as she is no longer able to hold control over her emotions. Her voice breaks, "From what I've been told, Ricky came home and found Doug passed out on the couch. Ricky didn't think anything of it because he sees him like that almost every day. A little while later, Ricky was heading out to go over to Walter's house. He tried to wake Doug up to tell him, but he

223

wouldn't budge. Ricky got scared and called 9-1-1. When the paramedics weren't able to get him to respond to anything they tried, they took him to the hospital. There, they worked on him, but they were never able to revive him. From preliminary results it looks like he died of alcohol poisoning. I have Ricky here with me now. I couldn't let him stay there alone. I wasn't going to leave him there; he's family to us."

David lowers his voice as he tries to fight back his own emotions, "As far as I'm concerned, I'll adopt Ricky if it comes to that. He's a good boy, and he's been a damn good friend to Jeremy. How did you get the hospital to release Ricky to you?"

"I...I...put in a phone call to the mayor." She continues, talking quickly, "The hospital wouldn't release him to me because we aren't family. They were going to put him somewhere, and I just couldn't allow that to happen. So, I called the mayor and told him everything. He said he would take care of it. A little while later, they released Ricky into my custody."

Jessica continues, "David, you wouldn't believe how incredible these kids have been. Once they found out, they all flocked here. Since Ricky has been here, Zach, Larry, Walter, Jeff, Brett, Carlos, and Jake have all been piled in the living room. I told them that they didn't have to stay, but that didn't matter. They want to be here for their friend. They really are such a great group of boys."

David thinks long and hard before saying his next words, "I think I'm going to tell Jeremy tomorrow and let him have tonight. I know Jeremy. He's going to want to come home right away if he finds out. So, when I do tell him in the morning, if he wants to head back home instead of practicing that final day, I'm fine with it."

David can hear the sorrow in Jessica's voice as she continues, "Ricky looked so sad the whole car ride here. I think this is really killing him on the inside. I mean, he's already lost his mother and now this. How much can one child take?"

David's mind is rapidly going through all of the possible scenarios of what could happen next to Ricky. His father's passing is really going to complicate things because Ricky doesn't have any family, other than his father, that lives in the area. Both sets of grandparents passed away years ago. He has one uncle that lives out in Oregon somewhere that he never talks to. Outside of that, all he has are Jeremy and his parents.

"I just wanted you to know everything that is going on here. This way, you don't walk into a situation when you get back that you know nothing about."

"I appreciate that, honey. And seriously, I'm glad you took Ricky in. I wouldn't want it any other way. Just do me one favor, order some pizza or something before those kids eat us out of house and home."

Jessica smiles, "I'll make sure I do that. I miss you."

"I miss you, too; love you. I'll see you soon."

David hangs up and slides the phone back into his pocket. He is not looking forward to telling Jeremy what he had just heard, but he has resolved himself to wait until the next morning to fill him in on the sad news. He reminds himself of something Jeremy had said before. This group of boys really is something extraordinary. They are more than just friends; there is a much stronger bond there.

David looks up to see the sun beginning to set. Oranges and reds fill the sky. He just sits there watching the sun go down below the horizon. He marvels at the wonder and majesty of nature for a little while before eventually walking to the waiting area.

"Are you sure you know where you are going, Dad?" Jeremy's voice sounds impatient as he strains his eyes to see the GPS on his father's phone. They have been driving for over an hour already and the anticipation is getting to him. "Yes, I know where I am going. Well, I don't, but the GPS knows where it is going. According to this, we will be there shortly."

Thoughts race through Jeremy's head about what the house will be like. Will it be bigger than Walter's? Will he have cool jerseys and stuff hanging on the walls?

David's phone beeps and a voice springs to life, "You have reached your destination." The two look up and see a massive building. "He must live in a condo" says David. "Let me take a look at the message again. Yup, he lives in unit number 21."

David drives the car down the road that heads towards the condo building. In front of him is a massive gate with a small booth on the left hand side. As they approach, a man wearing a dark grey security uniform comes out of the building. "Who are you here to see, sir?"

David smiles at the man, "Hello, we are guests of Brady Clark's. He invited my son and me to dinner tonight."

The security guard looks at David and then Jeremy. "Let me check my list." He turns and stomps back to the little security hut. He comes back with a clipboard. On the clipboard is a sheet of white paper with a list of names on it, some of which have been crossed out. "What are your names?"

"My name is David Savage, and this is my son, Jeremy." The security guard follows the names down the list with his pen until he arrives at their names, "Here you are. Sorry about all the fuss, but our guests require the utmost privacy."

David smiles, "Not a problem at all; you're just doing your job." The security guard thanks David for his patience and walks back to the hut. He flips a switch, and the gate starts to swing open. David eases his foot down on the accelerator, propelling the car forward. A large sign to the right of the driveway read units 1-9 with an arrow towards the right, units 10-19 with an arrow facing left, and units 20-29 with an arrow pointing forward. They drive past some of the most impressive cars either of them have ever seen up close. "Dad, did you see that? That's the new Ferrari, and look over there, it's a Lamborghini! And next to that is an Aston Martin! This is insane!"

David drives the car onward until he sees unit 21. He pulls up to the unit and parks next to a brand new Corvette Sting Ray. Jeremy gets out of the car and walks around the Corvette. "This thing is beautiful, redesigned this year. Isn't it incredible, Dad?"

David has to admit, although they had just driven by some unbelievable-looking cars, this one has a special place in his heart. To him, there is nothing quite as sweet as the all-American muscle car. The Corvette is the best example of that. He felt that, no matter what you like in a car, this one has it. Tons of power, gorgeous lines, cool features, it has it all.

A voice behind them makes them both turn around, "Pretty sweet, huh? I just picked it up a few days ago. Love the color combo on this one." Brady walks out of the condo and over to where they are standing. "From your reactions, I take it you two are car junkies like me?"

"I have a poster of this exact car on my wall at home," says Jeremy. "It's so cool that I get to see this particular model up close!"

"I had it special ordered from the factory. This ZR-1 has a beast of an engine in it, but, naturally, I had to juice it up a bit."

David is giddy, acting like a kid in a candy store, "This is one beautiful machine."

Brady produces a set of keys from his pocket, "Why don't you two go for a quick spin in it? I trust you, and if not, that's why we pay for insurance right?"

David laughs nervously, "Thank you for the offer, but we couldn't do that. You barely know us. I can't just take your car out like that."

"Please, I insist. I get to drive it whenever I want. Go ahead, have a little fun." He tosses the keys to David who catches them with one hand. "Seriously, go ahead. Try to be back in like twenty minutes. The food's almost done."

Brady closes the door. Jeremy and his father sit there looking at each other. "What should we do?" asks David.

"What do you mean? We should take the car out, that's what we should do! You heard him. He wants us to take it."

"I know what he said, Jeremy, but this is an expensive car. The kind that, if something happens, your mother and I can't replace."

"Do you think Brady Clark is worried about that? Like he said, that's why you have insurance. Besides, if he feels like it, he could buy fifty of these things! Let's go!"

Although David knows it isn't the best idea, he just can't help himself. This is the opportunity to drive one of the best made cars in the world, and he is not going to pass up on that chance. "If your mother finds out, she's going to kill me. But, you only live once. Get in!"

About fifteen minutes later, they arrive back at the security hut. This time, the guard recognizes them right away. "This isn't the same car you drove in with, right?"

"No, it most certainly is not!" says David. The guard laughs and allows them to pass through. They drive down to unit 21 and park. Jeremy takes a look at his father, "Dad that was incredible! Man this thing can really fly!"

David doesn't reply immediately to his son. He sits there for a moment, caressing the steering wheel. He knew the car was going to be fast, and he knew the brand new car would handle with precision. However, the ride surpassed all of his lofty expectations.

After a few seconds pass he looks at his son and smiles, "That was pretty cool wasn't it?" Jeremy bounds out of the car and makes his way to the front door. He knocks.

"Come on in!" comes the response from within.

Jeremy opens the door. The condo is much larger than he thought it would be from the outside. It runs the entire length of the building, stretching all the way out to a grass field in the back. The floors are a beautiful intermingling of deep and lighter reddish hues, which Jeremy later finds out, is a wood called Brazilian Cherry. To the right, there is a fireplace with a massive television hanging over it. Around the fireplace and stretching all the way up to the ceiling is beautiful stone work which accentuates the floors perfectly.

To the left is an enormous kitchen, which is where Brady is busily preparing the night's feast. The countertops are made out of some sort of stone that is the same coloring as that around the fireplace. Jeremy figures that it is perhaps granite or something similar to it. There are stainless steel appliances, a center island that houses a six-burner stove top, and, in the back, a full length dining room table.

Brady is working hard in the kitchen. He has a cloth slung over a shoulder, what looks like a peppermill in his right hand, and a large spoon in the other. "So, what did you guys think of the car? I'm assuming you brought it back in one piece?" he says with a grin.

"Mr. Clark, that car is amazing. Thanks for letting my dad and me drive it!"

"No problems, little Buddy, and please, just call me Brady. When people call me Mr. Clark it actually makes me feel sort of uncomfortable. What did you think, David? She have enough power for you?"

David still has a smile plastered on his face that stretches from ear to ear. Although he tries to shake it, he just can't get rid of the feeling of complete exhilaration just yet. "That is one impressive ride. I still can't believe you let us borrow it."

Brady tosses a few spices into the pan and stirs, "Not a problem, really. I don't want to sound arrogant, but if you did crack the car up, it's not like I couldn't afford to get another one tomorrow."

231

"See, I told you, Dad," said Jeremy, "money is no big deal to Brady Clark; he's got tons of it!"

Brady just chuckles, "Well, I don't go around boasting about it, but it's not like he's wrong, I guess. The last contract I signed will basically set me up for the rest of my life and probably another one after that."

Jeremy walks into the living room and looks around. It seems much like any other he has been in before. Then, he turns to the left and nearly faints. The room expands past the living room, opening up into one massive open space, which Jeremy couldn't readily tell from the doorway. He knows right away this is going to be his favorite room in the house. "Dad, you've got to see this!"

David looks over at Brady who is smirking, "I think he found my man room. When you're a bachelor such as myself, you get to decorate your house any way you want. When you see it, you'll know what I mean."

David follows his son's voice and walks up next to him. In the center of the room is a beautifully ornate pool table. On the walls hang all the former jerseys Brady has worn, including high school, college, professional, and all-stars. He also has autographed jerseys of his favorite players and a glass case that has signed basketballs, baseballs, a hockey stick, and footballs. There are four massive flat screen televisions on the walls and speakers everywhere. Also, bolted to the wall is a pool stick holder which holds five pool sticks and a dart board next to it.

David thinks that this is the ultimate bachelor pad. He yells out, "This is the greatest room I've ever seen."

"I thought you guys might like it; everybody does. We can hang out in there after dinner. Right now, food's ready. Let's eat!"

David and Jeremy speak to each other in hushed tones about how incredible the room is as they make their way to the large dining table and sit down. Brady puts out what he has cooked: filet mignon, sautéed onions and mushrooms, mashed sweet potatoes, and fresh bread. He sits down, unfolds his napkin, places it on his lap and slides in his chair. "Hungry?"

"Can I ask you something?" asks Jeremy.

"Shoot," replies Brady.

"You have so much money, why are you cooking your own food?"

"I get asked that a lot by my guests. To tell you the truth, I like cooking. I find it relaxing. My mother always told me that it was important that I know how to cook, so I learned from watching her when I was little. Plus, I eat out all the time during the season, especially when we're on the road. So, I like to eat as many home-cooked meals as I can in the off-season."

Jeremy already idolized Brady Clark; now he thinks that he is the coolest person on the planet. He is so down-to-Earth and nice. To go

233

along with that, he is the best player in the league, has an awesome house, and ridiculous cars; he has it all. Jeremy begins to wonder if he works hard enough, could he be like Brady Clark? Could he be better than him?

The three eat until their plates are completely clean. "Brady, that was incredible. You sure are one heck of a cook!" says David.

"Thanks. Like I said, I learned from watching the best, my mother. If you think that was good, you should have one of her meals someday."

After dinner, Brady leads them into what he refers to as his, 'man room' and they play pool and talk for hours. In spite of the fact that Jeremy is hanging out with his hero, his eyes begin to get heavy. His father, noticing this, puts down the pool stick that is in his hand. "You know, I think we should be heading out soon."

"You guys can crash here if you'd like, it's no problem" says Brady.

"Thanks, but all of our stuff is back at the hotel, and Jeremy has to be up early again tomorrow for camp."

Brady walks Jeremy and David to the door. "Jeremy, don't forget what I said before, text or call whenever you want someone to talk to. Make sure you listen to your parents. They only want what's best for you. Also, if you've got friends that you trust now, my advice would be to keep them close. As you go through high school, you'll find out that people can be a little too much at times, and as you get better, everyone is going to want to be your best friend. I've been through it all; I can help guide you through those tough times."

"Thanks Brady, I will definitely keep in touch. Thanks for tonight too; this was the best day of my life!"

Brady holds up a hand and Jeremy slaps him a high five. David thanks him again and they walk out the door.

Brady shuts the door and slowly walks to the living room. He sits down heavily on the couch, finds the remote, and turns on the television. He thinks back to the phone call he had earlier. The person on the other end of the line had finally called in a favor from him; a favor that Brady thought had been long overdue. It seemed pretty simple. Get close to some boy named Jeremy that is attending the camp this week and advise him to stay close to his friends when going to high school, which is something Brady thinks is true anyway. Although his initial reason for inviting the kid and his father over was in response to the request, he had actually grown to like Jeremy and his father in the short amount of time they have spent together. He really does want to help Jeremy and truly feels that he can help guide him through some of, what he knows will be, the toughest years of Jeremy's life.

Brady has been through a lot in his life. His father left when he was only a little boy, so he never had a male role model to look up to. His mother was incredible: working two jobs and somehow finding a way to make it to every game he ever had, but she knew nothing about sports or the way people would react as he continued to improve. He

235

didn't have someone on his side telling him to watch out for things or to hang on to the friends that he had, because once you get big, it's really tough to figure out who your true friends are.

As he sits on his couch watching sports, he vows that he will help make sure that Jeremy does not end up like him. When he was in high school, he sky-rocketed to the top of the college recruiting class, but he also lost every friend he ever had. As he moved through high school, he began to think that he was too good for all of his friends. Eventually, one by one, they stopped calling.

As a superstar, everyone wants to be around you, and Brady loved it; at least, he thought he did. When he got to college, it was even crazier. The parties got bigger, the nights got longer, and he got farther and farther away from the kid he used to be. Before he knew it, he was here. Granted, he is mightily successful on the grid iron, but he is pretty lonely too.

When he made it to the pros, he went out with lots of women. Any time he was out, guys would pay for his dinner or drinks, but it was all superficial because they already knew who he was. He couldn't get a true read on anyone anymore. Did they like him because he is a superstar, or did they like him for who he is? He couldn't tell anymore, and it drove him nuts.

So, one day, he just stopped. He stopped going out, stopped all the craziness that was his life. He is not going to let the same thing happen to Jeremy. So, he will be there. If he calls, he'll talk to him, and

236

really talk to him. He will be a true friend to Jeremy and tell him how important it is to stay grounded. He will let him know that the decisions he makes now, no matter how trivial they may seem, will have a massive impact on his future.

Brady continues to think about all of these things as his eyes start to close. His head slowly slides down the couch, and eventually rests on the seat next to him. He feels his body let go and drifts off into a deep sleep.

David turns the car into the parking lot and cuts off the engine. He rubs his eyes and looks over at his sleeping son. It was the right decision to not tell him about Ricky's dad until tomorrow. Jeremy had said it himself; it had been the best day of his life. He softly puts a hand on Jeremy's shoulder and shakes him lightly, "We're here. Come on, let's go get some sleep."

Jeremy opens one eye and then the other. He is completely exhausted. He opens the car door and stumbles out into the cool night air. He takes in a deep breath and follows his father up the stairs. David opens the door and Jeremy walks right past him and flops onto the bed. He is asleep in a matter of seconds.

David changes his clothes. He goes into the bathroom and brushes his teeth. He shuts off the light and lies down on the bed and stares at the ceiling. He tries to think of how he is going to break the news to Jeremy. Maybe he should wait until after the practice is over to tell him. No, that would be no good. It has already been a number of hours since he found out, and he knows that Jeremy will want to be there for his friend. He will just have to tell him first thing in the morning; there's simply no way around it. David leans over and checks to make sure the alarm is set. Once he confirms it is, he rolls over and falls fast asleep.

20

The alarm beeps noisily in the small hotel room. David wearily whacks at it until it stops making noise and flops onto his back. It is time to tell Jeremy. He looks over, Jeremy hasn't even moved. He gets up off the bed and walks over to his son. He puts a hand on Jeremy's shoulder and shakes him, "Jeremy, it's time to get up."

Jeremy stretches, kicking the blanket off of him in the process. "What time is it, Dad?"

"It's a little before seven. But, you and I need to talk before you get up."

Jeremy looks quizzically at his father, "What's up? Is something wrong?"

David takes a seat on the bed, "Something's happened back home. I found out yesterday, but I didn't want to tell you because I didn't want it to ruin your night."

Jeremy starts to feel nervous. He shoots up. "Is it Mom?"

"No, your mother's just fine. It's Ricky's dad. Apparently, he had a little too much to drink again. This time, it was more than the usual."

Jeremy wipes the gunk out of the corners of his eyes. He isn't surprised at all to hear that Ricky's dad has been drinking too much. "How bad is it this time?"

"Bad, it's real, real bad this time." David's voice trembles a bit, "He's…Jeremy, Ricky's dad passed away yesterday from what they think is alcohol poisoning. They tried to work on him, but he was too far gone."

The news hits Jeremy like a freight train. He knows that Ricky's dad has been drinking a lot, but this? As he fights to process the information, he becomes worried about his friend. Although Ricky often gives off the impression that he doesn't care about anything and that nothing ever bothers him, Jeremy knows that isn't the truth. "Where's Ricky? Is he ok? He doesn't have any family other than his dad-at least, none that he actually talks to."

"Ricky's fine. He's with your mother."

"So, what happens to Ricky?"

"Your mother signed some paperwork saying that we would take care of him for now. I guess it really freaked him out when he wasn't able to wake up his dad, which makes sense. Can you imagine finding me or your mother passed out and not being able to wake us up? Then, later finding out that his father did not make it just made everything that much worse."

Jeremy doesn't even need to think; he just reacts, "I want to go home. When can we fly out?"

"I haven't looked to see if we can move our flights up a day. I wanted to talk to you first. Also, I want you to really think about this. You only have one day of camp left. Are you really sure you want to pass that up to go home? There's nothing we can do for Ricky other than to be with him, and I guess all the guys have been staying at the house since this happened."

"What do you mean?"

"Your mother said that since this has happened, all of your friends have been at the house staying with Ricky. She told them that they didn't have to stick around, but they just don't want to leave him."

That makes the decision to go home even easier for Jeremy. He looks his father square in the face, "Dad, if we can go home early, I want to go home. He's my best friend, and I want to be there for him. I play football every day of the week, but football isn't everything."

David smiles and wipes away a tear, "You're a great kid Jeremy and a good friend. Ok, let me see what I can do." David gets up off the bed and walks over to the dresser. He unzips his bag and pulls out his laptop. He presses the button to turn it on and the screen springs to life. He waits for the computer to boot up and then clicks the internet icon. He searches the airline's website to see if there is an earlier flight that they can take.

"It looks like there are a few flights that leave for home early this afternoon, but we may have to take a connecting flight. Let me call the airline, explain our situation, and see if there's anything they can do to help us."

David finds his phone and punches in the number for the airline that is displayed on the computer screen. While he does this, Jeremy gets up out of bed and begins to pack his bag. The majority of his stuff is still back at the dorm room, but he puts together what he can. He balls up the clothes he wore last night and crams them in the bag, along with whatever else he has with him.

While he continues to pack, his thoughts drift back to last night. What a night it had been; what a day yesterday had been. He wouldn't have changed a single thing about any of it. He still couldn't believe that he had eaten dinner with Brady Clark. More than that, Brady wanted to be a mentor to him. Then, everything got flipped upside down this morning. Now, he is rushing to get all his stuff together to cut his trip short and head back home because his friend needs him. It shocked Jeremy to see how fast twenty-four hours can change things completely.

David thanks the man on the phone repeatedly and ends the call. "I would definitely fly this airline again any time. I told them about our situation and they are more than willing to help us out. We now have a direct flight home that leaves here at noon. So, we need to get moving. We've got to get back to the facility and grab your stuff, get to the airport, and drop off the car by then."

David finishes packing. He shoulders his lap top case and picks up the handle on his rolling suitcase, "Got everything, Jer?"

Jeremy checks the room one last time, "Yeah, I'm good to go."

David tosses his and Jeremy's bags into the car and drives over to the main lobby of the hotel. "I'll be right back. I just need to check-out. It should only take a moment or so." David hops out of the car and jogs to the front door. A few minutes later, he reappears. He slides into the driver's seat, and they speed off.

The coaches are shocked when they learn that Jeremy is leaving a day early. The head quarterbacks coach, Mel Branderson, makes it a point to find Jeremy and his father before they leave the facility. As Jeremy is placing the last of his belongings into his suitcase, a light knock is heard from the dorm room door. David gets up and opens the door to find Coach Branderson holding a wooden rectangular object in his hands. "Hello Mr. Savage, Jeremy, I just heard that you guys had to head out of town early. Something about a family emergency, is everything all right?"

Mel Branderson wasn't the type to show emotion. In fact, he often wondered if he actually had any emotions at all, other than a pure love for football. Throughout the week, he had gotten to know and respect Jeremy. More than that, he had actually grown to like him. The kid has tremendous talent and he takes every word you say to him to heart. He makes it a point to learn from any mistakes that he makes. It's the type of make-up in an athlete that you just can't teach. It's the kind of stuff that makes a champion, a champion. Mel feels very confident that Jeremy has *it*.

David answers Mel's question, "Yes, everything is fine. We just really need to get home to help a family friend. Thank you very much for asking."

243

Mel takes a step forward into the room, "Do you mind if I come in for a moment?"

"We really don't have a lot of time. Our flight is at noon," says David.

Mel takes a tentative step into the room, "This will only a take a second, I promise. He looks from David to Jeremy, "Well, this isn't exactly how we wanted to do this, but here it goes." Mel extends the rectangular object towards Jeremy indicating for him to take it. "Jeremy, every year we give out awards at the camp. We give them out for best at each position as well as best overall performer. On behalf of myself and the other coaches, we want to present you with the best overall performer at the Direct Athletics Performance Camp Award."

Jeremy takes the award from Mel and holds it in front of him, gazing over every feature of the plaque. He can't believe it. The last twenty-four hours have presented him with a whirlwind of emotions, ranging from the highest of highs to absolute lows. To be presented with the best overall performer award is a huge deal. Some of the best professional players have won this award before him, including Brady Clark.

Mel extends his hand to Jeremy, "First off, congratulations on the award. It's a major accomplishment. I'm sure I don't need to tell you what caliber of player it takes to win an award like this." Jeremy shakes the hand as Mel continues, "Listen Jeremy, I just have to tell you that you may be the best I've ever seen at your position, and I've seen a lot of great ones. You keep up that superior attitude you have and work ethic, and I'm sure one day, I'll be watching you on television. Just remember the little guys like me when you're a superstar."

Jeremy's cheeks redden at the coach's praises. "Thanks, Coach. This really means a lot.

"You've earned it. When you get home, put all the things you've learned here to good use. Kick some butt this season."

"Yes, sir," said Jeremy. Mel shakes David's hand and walks over to the door. He pauses and turns back, "You've got the skills to go all the way, Jeremy; of that, I'm sure. Keep your focus and make good decisions. If you do, you'll be playing on Saturdays in four years and Sundays after that." With that, he was gone.

David and Jeremy grab the rest of Jeremy's things and exit the room. "Hold on, Dad. There's one more thing I have to do." Jeremy puts down his bag and walks over to the desk. He searches around and finds a piece of paper and a pen and starts to write:

Jackson,

Thanks for being such a cool roommate. I've really learned a lot from you. Have a great year this year. I hope you play really well. Don't forget, you said that you were going to come and visit me during one of your school vacations, and I'm looking forward to that. I also can't wait to visit you in Florida sometime, maybe during the winter break we get from school. I think you're really going to like some of my crazy friends and that we will have a lot of fun.

245

Call or text me sometime soon. You have my number,

    Jeremy

Jeremy goes over to Jackson's bed and places the note by the pillow. He turns, picks up his bags, and heads out the door.

The flight lands and jostles Jeremy awake. They have been in the air for nearly five hours and the flight has taken all of the energy out of him. When the door finally opens, Jeremy and his father make their way slowly off the plane and down the ramp. They look to the board, find where their luggage is going to be, and walk over to the carousel. David looks at his watch which reads 5:30 P.M. "I guess I should change my watch back. It's definitely not 5:30 here." David switches his watch to read 8:30 P.M.

The conveyor starts to spin. They locate their luggage and pull it off the belt. David phones the shuttle service company to inform them that they have arrived. They tell him that they will be there to pick them up in about fifteen minutes. David and Jeremy take their bags outside and wait. Jeremy stretches, and looks up into the night sky. The space above him is completely black and the warm summer air is incredibly thick, almost suffocating.

The shuttle arrives and takes them to their car. From there, it is about an hour and a half ride back home.

The noise from the garage door alerts Jessica to their homecoming. She walks over to the door and opens it. David and

Jeremy take off for her, leaving their bags behind. Jeremy gives his mom a big hug, "Where's Ricky?"

"He and the other boys are in the basement. I think they are all sleeping down there. Why don't you go and see."

Jeremy gives her a kiss on the cheek, "Thanks, Mom, for everything." He gives her one last hug and then sprints for the basement. As soon as Jeremy runs past Jessica, David is there. He too gives her a big hug and a kiss. "What a week. Jess, I feel like I've been saying this a lot lately, but you're never going to believe this."

"After what happened to you two last night, I think, at this point, I'll believe basically anything you tell me."

David reaches into the car and pulls something out, "Check this out." David hands it to Jessica, who takes it in her hands and looks at it.

"I'm not sure what I am looking at here. It says best overall performer. So, I'm guessing Jeremy won this at camp this week or something?"

David puts his arm around Jessica and the two walk into the house together. "Yes, Jeremy won best overall at camp. He was picked by the coaches as the best player out of the greatest collection of football players for his grade in the entire country. Not just at his position, but the best overall. When we were about to leave, one of the coaches went out of his way to find us and gave that to Jeremy. He also told him that he was the best he's ever seen, ever. I'm telling you, Jess, this camp has really opened up my eyes. I knew he was good; everyone knows he's good. But, he very well might be other-worldly. Like, he may grow up to be the best that ever played."

Jessica puts her hands on the sides of David's face and kisses him. "Listen, I'm happy about all of this stuff, really, I am. But, there are other things going on right now that are a little bigger than a plaque. Are you one hundred percent sure that you're fine with Ricky staying here? Before you answer, I want to let you know that the mayor called a little while ago. He told me that if we want Ricky, he can make it happen for us, no strings attached."

David doesn't need any time to think, "I'm with you all the way. He's like our own, and I wouldn't want to see Ricky get bounced around."

"Good." Jessica wraps her arms around David's shoulders and gives him another kiss. "I knew I married you for a reason."

"Of course you did, my ravishing good looks, no? Or perhaps my undeniable charm?"

Jessica laughs and shakes her head, "I think that you should just stop while you're ahead. How about you go get the bags from the car and bring them inside. I'll make us a pot of coffee."

Jeremy can tell that the lights are off in the basement as he quietly walks down the stairs. A soft glow emanates from the television, serving as the only source of light as he reaches the bottom of the stairs. He looks around the room to find Ricky, Larry, Zach, Jeff, Walter, Brett, Carlos, and Jake all passed out at varying angles and spots

248

between the floor and the two couches. Then it hits him. Just like Jackson had told him it would, he knows what his decision is going to be. Looking around the room, he knows where he wants to play next year and the next three years after that. He has been racking his brain day and night, and now, the solution seems so simple that it actually causes him to laugh out loud a little. As he does so, Ricky's eyes open.

"Hey, what are you doing back? You're mom said that you weren't supposed to come home till tomorrow."

Jeremy steps over sleeping bodies until he finds a little spot on the floor near Ricky. He sits down and crisscrosses his legs. "I heard about your dad and wanted to come right home. I can't believe you didn't call or text me."

"I didn't want to bother you while you were away. Plus, look at all the support I've got around here."

Jeremy punches Ricky in his leg, "I wanted to be here for you."

Ricky smiles and nods his head up and down slowly, "You know, it was probably the scariest thing I've ever seen in my life. He just wouldn't move no matter what I did. When they told me he died, I just went completely numb. I think I'm still sort of numb now, like it didn't really happen or something." As the words gradually fall out, tears form in Ricky's eyes and begin to gently stream down his cheeks. Jeremy sits there and does what a best friend should do, he listens. He doesn't say anything; he just listens as Ricky tells him what happened in detail and exactly how it felt for *him*: free from judgment, free from interruption. Jeremy knows that it would have been hard for Ricky to tell any of the other guys precisely how he felt. Although the connection between all of the friends is extremely tight, there is just a different level between Ricky and Jeremy. They are more like brothers.

Ricky finishes telling his story. "Hey, that's enough of this sappy crap. How was the week? It must have been pretty awesome there."

Jeremy thinks that this may be a welcomed distraction for Ricky, "It was pretty sweet. Guess who I had dinner with last night."

"I don't know, you're dad?"

Jeremy rolls his eyes, "Yeah, my dad and one other very famous guy. A guy that also happens to be our favorite player."

Ricky shoots up out of his seat, "No way. There's no way that you hung out with Brady Clark. That's impossible."

The grin on Jeremy's face says it all. He doesn't even need to say one word.

"What! How did that happen! You've got to tell me everything, and I mean everything! Don't leave out a single detail, not one!"

Ricky's shouting wakes up some of the other guys. Zach opens one eye, "Savvy, is that you?"

"Yeah, it's me. I'm back."

Walter rolls over, "Hey, Savvy, when did you get here?"

One by one, the guys all wake up and Ricky recounts what Jeremy has started to tell him. Jeremy tells the entire story of last night

250

to the guys, who are mesmerized by the entire tale. He shows them Brady's number in his phone with incredible pride and some of the photos he took last night while he was there.

Not long after Jeremy is finished telling the story, all of them, including Jeremy, find a spot to lie down and drift off to sleep.

21

The next morning, Jeremy is the first to wake up. He stumbles over someone's foot and goes over to Ricky. He gives Ricky's body a little shove. Ricky slowly opens up his eyes, "What do you want, I'm still sleeping."

"I need to talk to you, but not here. Let's go take a walk." Ricky begrudgingly gets up and puts on his shoes. He follows Jeremy out of the house.

Jeremy checks over his shoulder and makes sure that they are a good distance away from the house. He is a little hesitant to tell Ricky what he is about to say, mostly because he is afraid that he may have to separate from his best friend in the whole world for the first time ever. He begins, "Listen, I want you to be the first to know. I'm going to go to Centerville next year. I had been unable to decide, but when I got home and saw all you guys together, I just knew I wanted to stay with all of our friends and go to Centerville."

Ricky stops dead in his tracks and sighs heavily, "You have no idea how happy I am to hear you say that. As you know, I was all in on St. Michael's from the start. Then, with everything that has happened with my dad and the guys, there is no way I want to be without them. I can't believe that none of them have left for even a second, not even Carlos, and he doesn't even know me that well."

"They really are great friends, aren't they?"

252

Ricky shoves Jeremy lightly, "No, *we* are all great friends, and I'm not going to be the one to break it up."

"Me either."

They continue to walk and talk for a while before eventually heading back to the house.

The two are gone for over an hour before they finally arrive back at the house. By the time they do, the other guys are all up and eating breakfast at the table. Zach is stacking his plate with a second helping of pancakes while Jeff is balancing a plate full of food on his head.

"See, I told you guys I could do it. No sweat."

Jeremy's mother yells at him from over the stove, "Jeff, I love you dearly, but would you mind taking my plate off of your head, please?"

Jeremy looks at Ricky, "Should we tell them together?"

"Tell us what?" asks Walter who is stuffing a third piece of bacon into his mouth without actually finishing chewing the first two.

"Nah, it's all you," says Ricky.

"Hey, you two, spit it out already. You're interrupting feeding time, not a good idea," says Zach.

Jeremy stares out at his friends and his parents. "Well, it's been a real difficult time lately for all of us, but especially Ricky. After a long talk, Ricky and I have decided that we are *both* going to go to

253

Centerville with you guys and see what we can accomplish together as a group."

"Yeah," says Ricky, "you guys have shown me that some things are more important than football. It's no secret that I was all-in on St. Michael's when I first got the offer. But, after all that's happened, there's no way I'd want to be anywhere else than with all of you." He begins to tear up a bit, "I lost my dad, but to tell you all the truth, it feels like I lost him a long time ago. Now, you guys are my family."

Walter gets up from the table and puts an arm around Ricky who fights to stifle back his tears.

Jeremy adds, "For me, when I got home and saw the way you all rallied round Ricky, I knew that this is just not something I can be without. You guys are the best, and I want to enjoy everything that's going to happen in high school with all of you, my true friends." said Jeremy.

Jeff stands up and walks over to Jeremy and Ricky, "I love you guys too." Jeff gives Jeremy a hug. "You too. Get over here." Jeff hugs Ricky as well.

Zach bolts out of his seat and also hugs both Jeremy and Ricky ferociously. "I knew it! I knew you guys weren't going to leave us."

Since Jeremy and Ricky had told him that they may be going to St. Michael's, Zach had been trying really hard to keep himself together. But, the truth is, he felt completely blindsided by the whole thing. He was starting to wonder if they were really as good of friends as he thought they were. There is no way that Zach, if given the same offer, would even consider leaving his friends behind to play somewhere else. Even though he felt that way, once he heard about Ricky's dad, he came running. To him, Ricky was his brother, and he needed him, just like Jeremy had needed him the night of the party. Right now, hearing that they are both going to stay, he feels like his beliefs have been re-affirmed. It isn't just in his head; these guys feel the same strong link as well.

David puts an arm around Jessica and whispers, "These kids are amazing. Once we are finished eating, I'll call the mayor and thank him for his help with Ricky."

"Yes, but I know you; you also want to tell him that Jeremy is going to go to Centerville, don't you?"

"No, I just want to thank him for all he did, that's all."

Jessica knows David can't keep anything a secret. One year for Christmas, David bought her a pair of diamond earrings in early October; she had them on her ears by Halloween.

"Ok dear, whatever you say."

"Hey Dad, do you mind getting Coach Fletcher's card for me? I want to call him and let him know. I'm sure Ricky is going to want to do the same, too."

"No problem, Jeremy. I'll grab it in a second." David cuts a large piece of pancake, carefully places a small piece of bacon on top of it, and heaves both into his mouth at the same time, enjoying every second of the exquisite flavors.

The group sits there, enjoying eating their breakfasts together, until all of the food is gone. The guys joke around with each other relentlessly, keeping the mood light. They listen to Jeremy, once again, tell them all about the night at Brady Clark's house.

Once everyone is done, Jessica looks around at all of the carnage. Although she had fed the boys before, she still can't get over the sheer enormity of the amount of food they can eat, especially Zach, who had finished off three full helpings. The boys clean off their plates and put them in the dishwasher, thanking and complimenting Jessica on her breakfast as they do so.

Once he is finished, David goes upstairs to grab his wallet and get the coach's card for Jeremy. While he is up there, he picks up the phone and dials.

"Hello, David. How are you this fine morning?"

"I'm very well, Mr. Mayor. How are you?"

"Please, I told you to call me Clinton. I'm doing ok this morning. How's that boy doing?"

"He's doing fine right now. Jessica and I can't thank you enough for everything. I don't know what I would have done if they tried to place Ricky in foster care. They just can't take him away from his friends."

256

"No trouble at all. Anything I can do to help a friend in need. You let me know if you need anything else regarding him."

"I will do that, because it looks like we may try to keep him ourselves. On a completely different note, I thought you might be interested to know that Jeremy just told my wife and me that he has chosen Centerville and so has Ricky."

The mayor typically gets what he wants, but this is an especially sweet victory for him. Even through the somber news of the boys' fathers' death, the mayor can't help but feel joy. He knows what this means for his future. Not only would this please his constituents, but it will also cement Centerville as a force to be reckoned with in the state for the next four years. On top of that, he gets to one-up that cocky Coach Fletcher. He grins to himself, "Well, that is great to hear, great indeed. I mean, I'm very sorry about Ricky's loss as well. David, I'm going to share this information with some of the gentlemen that you met the other night. I'd love it if you and Jessica could come to Pemberton tonight so we can discuss this matter further."

"Jess and I would love to join you at Pemberton. I want to make sure I tell you in person how appreciative I am of what you have done. What time would you like us to be there?"

"I'll see you both at six." With that, the mayor hangs up the phone.

David walks down the stairs with the coach's business card in his hand. He sees Jessica, "We have plans tonight. We are going to

257

Pemberton to have dinner with the mayor and some of our new acquaintances. I know it may not be the best time, but I want to show him how much we appreciate what he has done for us, and I'd rather do that in person."

"I completely understand, and I agree." Jessica rests her head on David's shoulder. "I just can't believe Doug's gone."

He kisses her forehead softly, "It's a terrible thing. I hope Ricky is going to be ok."

A little while later, David yells down to the basement, "Jeremy, I've got the card for you!"

Jeremy runs up the stairs from the basement, "Thanks, Dad."

David can hear shouting followed by loud banging coming from the basement, "Jeremy, what are you guys doing down there?"

"Oh, that. We took the game system from my room and brought it downstairs. Right now, Walter is destroying everyone in this new game Brett brought over. The guy is sick!" Jeremy takes the card from his dad's hand and walks back down the stairs to rejoin his friends.

"Ricky, I'm going to call Coach now. You want to come with me?" Ricky gives a quick nod to Jeremy while he continues to watch Walter demolish the competition, taking out each of their friends one-by-one. Walter's thumbs swirl around at an amazing rate and his fingers tap buttons all over the controller as he continues to dominate. He has a laser-like focus that can only be seen when he is playing video games.

While watching the show Walter was putting on, Jeremy sends a quick text to Lauren. It reads: "*Made up my mind. Going to Centerville, looks like we will be seeing a lot more of each other.*" Jeremy's phone vibrates a fraction of a second after he hits the send button: "*Glad to hear it, looking forward to rooting for you guys this season. You practicing today?*"

"*No, off till Monday. Want to get together later?*"

"*Sounds great! Text me when you're ready.*"

Ricky looks over Jeremy's shoulder and peeks at this phone, "Aww... that's so cute. You two love birds are getting together later?"

Jeremy shoves Ricky towards the door at the back of the room. The door leads to the backyard which Jeremy thinks will give them enough privacy so that they can make the call.

"Stop spying on me...let's go get this call over with. I'm not looking forward to it." Jeremy and Ricky walk out the door and into the blazing sunshine. Jeremy closes his eyes as to allow them to adjust to the incredible brightness. He waits for them to regulate. Once they do, he takes out his phone. He looks at the coach's business card and dials the number on the card. Jeremy pushes a button on the phone to turn on the speaker phone and waits. The call is picked up after two rings, "Hello, this is Robert Fletcher."

"Hi, Coach. It's Jeremy."

"Hi, Coach, It's Ricky. I'm on the call as well."

"Hello, boys. How are you this beautiful morning?"

The tone of coach's voice makes Jeremy feel a little guilty for what he is about to say. Jeremy is the first to speak, "Coach, this has been a really difficult decision for me to make, but I feel like I have really looked at all of my options and considered everything. Although I can't disagree with the fact that St. Michael's is superior to Centerville in virtually every way, I just don't feel like it's the best place for me."

On the other end of the phone there is pure silence. Robert Fletcher is used to getting anything that he wishes and any athlete he desires. He sits there speechless as he listens while Jeremy and Ricky continue to describe the reasons why they *aren't* going to attend St. Michael's.

The coach squeezes the phone in his hand as he listens, shocked at the audacity of these two ungrateful brats. Out of unbridled anger, he starts to speak before really calculating what it is that he wants to say. "Well, I'm sorry to hear that. I've got to say that I'm really not sure what you two are thinking about with this decision. Didn't you see what happened at that scrimmage? Centerville is no match for top-tier talent in this state, and they never will be."

At that moment, Jeremy knows that his earlier suspicions had been true. It seemed awfully strange that there would be a scrimmage between Centerville and St. Michael's, seeing as there has never been a scrimmage between the two teams before.

"You know, Coach, I thought it was odd that we were scrimmaging St. Michael's. I'm now pretty sure that it was all orchestrated by you as a way of showing me what I would be in for if I chose to play at Centerville this upcoming season."

The tone of the coach's voice completely changes, "I can't confirm or deny what you're saying. What I can tell you is that we stomped all over Centerville, just like we always do." His voice escalates as he continues to speak, irritation coursing through every word, "Just like we are going to stomp all over them this year with or without you two. You must think that you guys are pretty damn special, don't you? Think that you can take that crap bag of talent at Centerville and come and play with the big boys? Well, think again. What you saw at the scrimmage is just the beginning. I'm going to personally see to it that we don't just beat Centerville, but that we humiliate you when we play each other this season, and every other season after that!" The coach terminates the phone call, ending it abruptly.

"Wow! What a jerk!" says Ricky. "He's nothing like I thought he was."

Jeremy stares blankly at the phone in his hand, unable to comprehend what has just happened. He has never been spoken to like that in his entire life. Suddenly, a feeling begins to well up inside of him. His face contorts as he puts the phone back into his pocket. He forms fists with his hands. It is a feeling that Jeremy has never really felt before. He's angry. Not just the normal kind of angry that you go through on a day-to-day basis from goofy things that happen, but irate.

Jeremy bursts through the door, interrupting the game. The guys look up at him and see a completely different face from what they have ever seen before on Jeremy. Jeremy stomps over to the television and stands directly in front of it, blocking everyone's view of the screen. "Listen up, I've got something to say." His cheeks are burning red and his eyes are like stone. "We just got off the phone with Coach Fletcher, who I now know is a complete tool. Anyway, he thinks that everyone here sucks. He thinks that our team sucks and that it's always going to suck. Well, guess what, I don't care if it's the last thing we do together, but we are going to beat St. Michael's. We are going to practice day and night, weekends, holidays; I don't care if I have to practice in my sleep. It has now become my life's mission to beat that arrogant jerk's team."

Zach stands up very quietly, "I got your back. Whatever it takes, we are going to take them down." Zach walks over to Jeremy and stands next to him showing a complete sign of support. One by one, the rest of the guys stand up. Fire burns in Jeremy's eyes. He has never felt this way before. He looks from face to face at each of his friends. He wasn't going to let them down. He wasn't going to fail. He was going to win, and win big.

David and Jessica arrive at Pemberton. They walk through the entryway and continue on to the same ballroom as before. The mayor is already there, talking it up with a number of members, most of which, David and Jessica had met the last time they dined at the club. Standing next to the mayor is a man that David does not recognize. The man looks to be in his late forties, with dark brown, combed-back hair. He has wide shoulders and a thick neck. He looks out of place amongst the other men surrounding him and seems to be completely disinterested in anything the group is discussing. As David and Jessica walk over, the mayor takes a few steps towards them and greets them. "David, Jessica, it's wonderful to see you both here tonight. I can't tell you both how excited we all are that Jeremy has chosen to go to Centerville High School. This is truly going to put us on the map! He puts his arms around David and Jessica and lowers his voice, "You know, your son has made some people here very happy. Like I said before, the membership here is just a taste of what is to come."

David ignores the mayor's last statement, "We just want you to know how much your help with Ricky means to us. Ricky's like a second son. We would do anything for him."

"Like I said before, no trouble at all."

The mayor spins around and beckons for the man that was standing next to him. "I'd like to be the first to formally introduce you to the newest member of the Centerville family. This is Sean Templeton, our new head football coach. Sean has been coaching at a five A football program in Southern Texas. It took some arm-twisting, but we have been able to procure him from his high school and bring him up here to coach the most talented quarterback in the country. At least, that's according to a few friends of mine at Direct Athletics Performance.

David, completely stunned by the introduction, looks curiously at the mayor, "Who do you know at the camp?"

"David, my friend, I have friends all over."

The coach is not interested in what the mayor is talking about. His only interest is in meeting Jeremy's parents. He shakes David and Jessica's hands, "It's nice to meet you both. I've heard a great deal about you son, and I'm looking forward to seeing what he can do on the field."

The mayor chimes in, "Soon enough, soon enough, indeed. I'm sure you will not be disappointed."

The coach continues, "To be honest, I'm really here because of two reasons: a phone conversation I had with my old friend, Mel Branderson and to work with, arguably, the best quarterback prospect in the country. When Mel tells me that Jeremy's the best he's ever seen, and he's seen them all, it piques my interest. This opportunity presented itself, thanks to the mayor. So, after a chat with Mel and looking at your reports, I had no problem moving to Centerville to coach what I now believe is an elite-level talent. "

The mayor claps his hands together, "This is going to be the perfect match. The best quarterback this town has ever seen, with the best coach money can buy." He casts his gaze on David, "I told you that Centerville is tired of playing second fiddle. There will be no more of that. Sean has an impeccable track record, and we have hired him to work solely as the coach. He won't be teaching any classes or anything

264

like that. He's here to do one thing and one thing only, and that's win. Now, David, why don't you and I have a seat with Mr. Templeton and inform him about our rival, the number one team in the state that *almost* got our boy?"

Epilogue

The first day of double-sessions has finally arrived. Waiting for the team, is the new coach that everyone has been hearing about. The team knows that he is some hot shot out of Texas. The coach stands there looking out at the faces before him. He scans each of them before he speaks, "I know what this school's past history is and, frankly, I don't give a damn. This is a new season, a new coaching staff, and we will have a new attitude. I hear that people around these parts don't think that we have a chance to do anything. They think that we're a bunch of losers, that we are always going to be losers. I've got some news for them; we are not going to be a below average team this year, gentlemen. We are not going to be an average team either. I won't accept average. I won't accept anything on my field other than absolutely everything that you've got. If you give me that, I guarantee you that we will be standing on top of the heap come the end of the season. It all starts with today. We will approach every drill, every practice, every tackle, every hit, every opportunity to prepare with the utmost urgency. If you do not feel like you are prepared to give this team that sort of commitment, then I'd rather we part ways now. Don't waste my time. Don't waste this team's time, because we have goals to accomplish. If you are truly ready, if you are willing to give me and this team everything you have inside of you, then follow me out onto that field." He turns and marches out onto the field. The team forms ranks behind him and trails closely behind.

The fire that has been ignited by Coach Fletcher has been burning inside of Jeremy ever since that day on the phone. Today, listening to the coach's words, that blaze has been transformed into a complete inferno. From the moment he first talked to Coach Templeton, or "Coach T" as he said to call him, Jeremy knew that this is a man that he could not only learn from, but one that is willing to do whatever it takes to get the job done.

Jeremy takes his place under center for the first time in his high school career. The practice has been going smoothly as Coach T's pep talk has really amped up the team. Jeremy looks from left to right and taps his foot. Carlos, the running back behind him, acknowledges the shift and sprints to the right side of the formation. He gets into position and sets his feet. Jeremy sets the play in motion as he takes the ball from the center and quickly goes through his progressions. As he makes his read, he is focusing on two things: the play and everything that Coach Fletcher had said to him. Jeremy is determined to make every single play count to its fullest. He looks off one of his receivers and sets his sights on Ricky, who is streaking deep. Jeremy sets his feet and unfurls his well-crafted throwing motion. The ball explodes out of his hand, tearing through the air in a perfectly tight spiral.

Coach T watches as Jeremy unloads a beautiful pass to his receiver. The ball is caught and taken the rest of the way for what would have been a sure touchdown. He blows his whistle, "Good, now let's run it again. This time, better. I need everyone on the field to run this play flawlessly in order for me to feel good enough to move on to the next play."

While on the surface it looks like the play was run to perfection, Coach T knows exactly what to look for when he is critiquing a play. He noticed that one of the receivers was out of position and a lineman completely missed a block. What he also noticed, is that Jeremy is the real deal. The hype around this kid wasn't blown out of proportion. The throw he just made was the type that college recruits specifically look for. More than that, the kid has an intensity about him that he fell in love with the first time he met him. Today, Jeremy has approached every single drill like it is life or death. Coach T knows that is the type of focus and determination he needs out of his best players. If the best players are the hardest workers, the other players will follow their lead.

Jeremy takes his place under center once again and calls for the ball. The ball is moved by the center into Jeremy's hands. A defender bursts through the line, headed straight for him. Jeremy spins past him and plants his feet. As he locks in on his target, his thoughts drift to playing St. Michael's in the upcoming season. Every throw has to be on point; there can be no exceptions. With this goal in mind, Jeremy takes aim, and lets it fly.

47112053R00161

Made in the USA
Middletown, DE
04 June 2019